A GIFT MORE PRECIOUS THAN GOLD

Midwest Distribution: Lincolnshire Court, Carol Stream, Illinois 60188

West Coast Distribution: SE Whalesong Drive, Depoe Bay, Oregon 97341

Additional BOOKS by A. J. Lactaoen
No Greater Blessing, Legacy of the Magi Book 2; A Testament of Love, Legacy of the Magi Book 3.

TO ORDER: Available on Amazon, Leadership Books and Book stores near you.
ONLINE SHOPPING: www.911seminars.com under Shopping/Books

LEGACY BOOKS are available at special quantity discounts to use as fundraisers, premiums, gifts or for use in corporate sales promotions. For more information, call toll free 800.721.8222; email: 911@911seminars.com or write The Independents Group Press, 7040 Hawaii Kai Drive #26435, Honolulu, HI 96825.

ISBN 978-0-9771577-4-7
Publisher's Cataloging-in-Publication Data

Lactaoen, A. J.
A Gift More Precious Than Gold
p.c. Includes bibliographical references and index.

ISBN 978-0-9771577-4-7

1. Inspiration 2. Historical 3. Religious – United States

Dedication

If you listen, sometimes you will hear the voices which point the way to important choices on your journey through life. Only rarely do the voices trumpet the call so clearly there is no doubt in your mind you are on the right path. I listened to that call and married the girl of my dreams. I dedicate this book to her for her love and devotion always. Caryn, you are my muse.

Love You!

Forward

There comes a time when children decide to leave the nest to go off on their own. Parents by virtue of being parents know that day will come and must prepare for it. Nevertheless, my wife insisted that we had not completed the task of instilling life's important lessons in our two boys a legacy of values as it were. So in typical fatherly fashion, I began sending our boys Jimmy and Jon, a series of memos with important advice which I entitled "Epistles from Dad." That it turns out was the model for the "Precepts of Happiness."

A Gift More Precious Than Gold

Prologue

"This is a collection of my manuscripts which I leave as a record of my passage through this journey we call life on earth. I leave it with all humility as an inheritance for my brethren… not to highlight any of my accomplishments but to leave the seeds of wisdom which can grow to fruition only with the passage of time… this is my wish for the generations to follow, this is my legacy… "

Μελχιορ
Magi

Chapter One:

The Invitation

"Professor Hamilton!" the voice cried out. Scott Hamilton, who was detailing a section of his last archaeological dig in Greece on the blackboard, turned quickly, expecting to see one of his students with arm raised in a query. Instead he was standing face to face with Henrietta Barrows, the Dean of the College of Arts and Sciences of Lehigh University.

"The President wishes to speak with you immediately!" With that said, Dean Barrows did a pirouette and heel toed off in a huff.

It must be important, thought Scott, if the Dean was sent as a messenger all the way across campus from the administration building to Drown Hall on Sayre Drive where the Classics Department had classrooms, offices and archaeological displays.

"Ladies and gentlemen, instructed Scott, we will continue our discussion on the myth of the Trojan Horse at our next meeting. Your assignment for tonight is to do research on the man who discovered the walls of Troy, one of the most eminent archaeologists of his day, Heinrich Schleimann. See you all on Wednesday."

As his students filed out of the classroom, Scott's thoughts turned to the reason he had been summoned by President Kelley. Hopefully it wasn't because of his comments at the last faculty committee meeting on departmental policy. Try as he might Scott couldn't shake the negative feelings he had about the College's new policy on tenure. No appointments to the rank of full Professor would be confirmed unless the department's approval was unanimous. If only one Professor did not like the way you conducted your class or the color of your suit, for that matter, he could effectively block even the most deserving educator's path to membership in the clubhouse. Politics! Even in the ivory halls of academia.

Still mired in deep thought about his undergraduate career and fraternity days at the University of Minnesota and how he fought against the inequity of the black ball system, Scott found himself in front of the administration building. Taking two steps at a time, he quickly covered the three flights up the ornate staircase, turned down the dark paneled hallway and stepped briskly through the open promenade to the executive offices.

"He's waiting for you, Professor," chimed Delia who was standing at the entrance to the main doorway.

"Thank you, Delia. You're looking lovely as usual today."

Delia blushed as she shooed Scott in with a wave of her hand, acknowledging the twinkle in his eye. Rumor had it that Delia Eichmiller was older than the 125 year storied campus building she roosted in through five administrations. Want to get through to the President? Only if you knew the way past Delia first..

"Come in, come in, Professor," President Jack Kelley exclaimed as he strolled over to grasp Scott's hand in his typical upbeat fashion. "Want to introduce you to Mr. Hartwell here who insisted on seeing you as soon as possible. Since he says he represents the Kincaid Trust, one of the biggest contributors to our Legacy Foundation as you know, I thought it best to interrupt your class. Knew you wouldn't mind, now do you, Scottie?" Beckoning to the chair closet to his massive rosewood desk, President Kelley motioned to Scott, "Sit down. Sit, sit."

Before Scott could move, the tall, heavy set Hartwell sprang forward to greet him.

"If you don't mind, Sir, would you please accompany me

downstairs? We have a car waiting." Without expecting a response, the officious Hartwell dressed nattily in an all black suit took Scott by the elbow and guided him to the door.

Looking up in surprise President Kelley stammered, "But I thought…that we were going to discuss…" The door shut promptly.

"Just a minute, Hartwell, what's this all about? Where are we going? I can't leave the campus yet. I have tutorials scheduled…,"complained Scott following his impervious guide out to the circular driveway behind the administration building.

Just then a Rolls Royce Limousine, an exact duplicate of the famous two tone yellow and brown classic vehicle in the movie "Arthur" pulled up to the curb and a freshly scrubbed young man dressed in a chauffeur's uniform smartly stepped up to open the rear door for his two passengers.

After settling comfortably in the plush leather upholstery, Hartwell offered the following. "Professor Hamilton, I understand that you are anxious to find out the purpose for this meeting. My instructions were to present this envelope to you personally and to await your answer.

Hartwell opened the leather briefcase he was carrying and extracted a large white envelope which he handed over to Scott. Looking at the silver haired stranger sitting opposite him in an automobile straight out of Hollywood, a broad smile spread across Scott's face. Yes, he finally figured it out. This was a set up by Statz, R. Joseph Statz, his old fraternity brother from Sigma Chi nicknamed the Prankster. Had to be.

As if he were reading his mind, Hartwell broke Scott's reverie, "No, Professor, this isn't a joke. Please open the envelope." Frowning, Scott did as he was told and pulled out the invitation embossed in antique gold and sealed in wax. Delicately handwritten in script were the letters RSVP.

Finding it difficult to make out the old English Script, Scott read slowly…

Professor Scott Hamilton,

You are among an elite group of people invited to attend a unique all expenses paid SYMPOSIUM on December 6-8 at the Waldorf-Astoria in New York.

Experts from your field of endeavor and other disciplines including representatives of education, business, psychology, medicine and science from around the world will be in attendance. To be sure, we guarantee that this will be a life changing experience. If you decide to accept our invitation, strict confidentiality is required. Any breach of this arrangement will effectively cancel your participation.

Reservations have been made for you and Mrs. Hamilton to check in on Friday night to enjoy a special dinner for two in one of the Waldorf's fine Restaurants.

The SYMPOSIUM begins Saturday morning at 9:00 A.M. sharp. Please give Hartwell your response before returning to the University.

The look of confusion must have been clearly evident on his face as Scott finished reading the cryptic invitation and implored Hartwell

"I have a bakers dozen to ask, he said hesitantly, but I assume you won't give me any answers, will you?"

Tapping on the see through window, Hartwell instructed the chauffeur to make the final turn back to the University Campus.

"All in good time, Professor, all of your questions will be answered at the Waldorf. Shall we expect you and Mrs. Hamilton?"

Scott opened the door as the vehicle stopped in front of Drown Hall, jumped out, and turned back to Hartwell and answered, "Wouldn't miss it for the world. See ya, Hart!"

Opening his office door, Scott wasn't at all surprised to find President Kelley waiting impatiently for his return.

'Well, will you tell me what the blazes is going on around here, Hamilton? I've got a University to run. I don't have time to be chasing after you and the likes of Hartwell. Well?"

Grabbing his brown worn-out leather briefcase and throwing the strap over his shoulder in one quick motion, Scott backed out of the doorway with his hands waving up in the air, the visibly irate President could scarcely make out the fast fading voice yelling "Can't talk now, got to tell Ellen the good news…"

Ellen Hamilton was her husband's number one fan and his closest confidante. She knew his strong qualities were his total dedication to teaching and his deep commitment to his students. Other colleagues had leap-frogged past Scott in the Classics Department's hierarchy on the strength of their research and publication. She dreaded the oft quoted 'Publish or Perish" mantra heard over and over at faculty socials. Of course she felt her husband's humiliation at being passed over by younger associates and knew his frustration at having his submissions rejected time and again by the Classical Journal and TAPA, a leading publication for Classicists. Ellen also knew that Scott's situation was due to his lack of motivation. His heart was not in publishing what he considered unnecessary minutiae.

"There it is, Scott, the Waldorf!" Scott smiled proudly as he watched his wife take in the outline of the famed Art Deco landmark. The Waldorf Astoria since 1893 epitomized the image of the 'Grand Hotel', a combination of luxurious elegance with the ultimate in amenities and guest services. And, in fact, Scott and Ellen spent their dream honeymoon at this five-star hotel. The trip from Nazareth had been just what they needed to take their minds off the day to day problems with the kids, the bills, the in-laws. This weekend away was the perfect respite.

Ellen had reacted wonderfully to the news of the Symposium and had their suitcases packed in record time awaiting the limousine which was sent by their hosts. Hartwell arrived exactly on time in the limo which Ellen had oohed and aahed over, deservedly so as it was their first ride ever in such an elegant carriage. It simply was not in vogue to splurge on such extravagant luxuries when the Hamiltons got married. Now the young people didn't think twice about the cost. It was the thing to do without question.

The Head Valet in top hat opened the limo door and addressed the couple by name. "Welcome to the Waldorf, Mr. & Mrs. Hamilton. Please proceed into the foyer where the concierge is expecting you. Our bellman will deliver your luggage directly to your room."

Walking through the elegant lobby brought back memories of shopping trips to New York over the holidays. The Waldorf was indeed one of New York's best people-watching venues. "What a wonderful feeling it was to be staying here again," Ellen mused, "even if just for the weekend."

"We are so happy to have you with us here at the Waldorf," the concierge greeted them warmly. "We have a special table reserved for you in your dining room at 8:00 tonight. Let me escort you to your room so you may freshen up. If you need anything or have any questions, our staff will be available at your convenience." Ellen glanced at Scott as their guide opened the double carved doors leading into their enormous suite. Just one look. No need for any words.

It was only 6:30 a.m. when Scott took the elevator down to the main lobby looking for the Peacock Alley dining room for a quick breakfast. Ellen was still fast asleep after a romantic dinner at the Inagiku Restaurant, the stylish and exotic New-Style Japanese restaurant at the Waldorf. They had been escorted into one of the exquisite tatami rooms usually reserved for VIP's. Needless to say the creativity and presentation of the meals was out of this world. The appetizers alone were worth the price. Crab roll with fried porcini mushrooms and roasted shallots; large shrimp filled with parma ham on saffron risotto. For her main dish Ellen selected the Sugar coated Long Island Duck on slow roasted onion quiche. Scott, always the meat eater, had the Grilled Buffalo Tenderloin with Cipolla Marmalade. Not the typical menu selection one would expect in a Japanese restaurant. Pacific Rim is what the maitre'd called it. The white chocolate cheesecake with caramelized macadamia nuts was the topping on a sumptuous dinner. Sampling the specialty beers at the hotel's Bull and Bear Bar after dinner along with a cozy dance brought a perfect evening to a close. If nothing else developed from this trip, Scott thought wistfully, the look of excitement on Ellen's face last night was memorable enough. Scott sipped on his second cup of coffee as he skimmed over the sports section of the morning New York Times. The New York Giants were making a run for the NFL championship so the news coverage was predominantly about football. Not being able to focus on anything in particular, Scott decided to venture outside the hotel for a short walk.

Enjoying the stroll along Park Avenue, Scott felt a sense of peace which had escaped him for so long. He didn't know why…maybe it was the anticipation of the symposium, or Ellen's obvious enthrallment with the whole experience, but deep down in his gut Scott knew something wonderful was about to happen.

Chapter Two:

The Symposium

As Scott reentered the Waldorf Astoria through the revolving glass door he noticed Hartwell pacing back and forth in the reception area. Obviously relieved when he saw Scott, Hartwell called out, "Professor! There you are. Your wife didn't know where you were. We can't be late for the start of the symposium, you know. Please follow me."

Continuing to talk while rushing through the lobby, Hartwell rambled on, "Don't worry about Mrs. Hamilton. She's scheduled to join the other spouses for a cruise in the harbor around Ellis Island up to the Statue of Liberty. They will also attend a special show at Radio City Music Hall and get to meet former Mayor Rudy at a reception for the New York Firefighters Association."

Excited by the prospect of discovering the reason for all the secrecy surrounding the invitation by the Kincaid Trust to this special event, Scott kept pace with the quick stepping Hartwell. Glancing at his watch when they stopped in front of the Presidential Boardroom, Scott thought they were early as it was only 8:45 a.m.

Hartwell knocked twice and a dour-faced looking butler opened the door and immediately announced in a booming voice, "Ladies and Gentlemen, please welcome Professor Scott Hamilton from Lehigh University, Pennsylvania."

As if on cue, everyone in the room stood in unison as Scott found himself escorted by the shiny bald headed butler to the only empty seat in the conference room. No wonder Hartwell had been so nervous, Scott was the last to arrive. Embarrassed, Scott sheepishly looked around the huge conference table to see if he recognized any of the other participants.

At exactly 9:00 a.m. the inner doors of the boardroom opened and a procession of bodyguards preceded an impeccably dressed handsome young man looking very much like a GQ ad in his double breasted Pierre Cardin. He spoke in a soft but commanding voice, "Good Morning, my friends. Welcome to our symposium. I am glad to see that all of the guests we invited decided to join us. I know you all have many questions and I promise that before you leave New York, you will have your answers."

Everyone around the room sat mesmerized. He continued, "Let us begin with introductions. My name is Arthur Kincaid III, executor of the Kincaid Foundation established by my great grandfather over one hundred and fifty years ago and which continues a tradition handed down by my ancestors. The primary beneficiaries of our trust funds are non profit educational institutions such as Lehigh University and other charitable organizations. Today, however, we will talk of different matters."

Looking around the room, he motioned for his assistant to hand a wireless mike to the pretty Asian lady sitting directly in front of him, then added, "Before we proceed any further, please do us the courtesy of introducing yourselves. Scott listened carefully as each of the guests sitting around the massive boardroom table stood up and addressed the group.

"Zao Shang hao. Wo jiao Chao Lin Dang Hong Kong."

"Guten Morgen. Ich heibe Gustave Kreiger auf Germany. Sehr erfreut."

"Buenos dios. Que tal mucho gusto. Me llamo Ceasar Ruiz

donde Spain."

"Ohaiyo gozaimasu. Jiko shokai shitemo ii desuka? Watakushi no name wa Makiko Watanabe desu Japan."

"Bon jour. Je m'appelle Franz Robelle, France."

"Good Day. William MacCary here from England."

Scott took his turn introducing himself, handed the mike over to the striking woman with the beautiful bronze complexion on his left, then sat down scribbling the names of the attendees in his notes. He recognized one of the people seated at the head table in front of the room but none of the guests around the conference table. Many spoke in their native tongue though it was understood that everyone spoke English as well. In his own field of Classics, Scott had been required to have a reading knowledge of German and French as well as Hebrew, so he assumed that the assembled group would be multi lingual as well. The introductions continued.

"Hi Y'all, my name is Nancy, Nancy Demray from the Peachtree State of Georgia."

"Zdrostvuytye minya zavut Irena Kasparov, Russia."

"Martin Steinberg, Israel."

"Talofa! I am Numi Tafasau from Tahiti."

"Namashe mai, Sister Carol Ann from India, God Bless you all."

"Omar Bodurin, I am from Egypt."

"Magandang unaga Wilma Ortale. I represent the Phillippines."

"Buon giorno. Mi chiamo Roberto Sellitto de Italia. We are so, how you say, 'happy', to be here in New York."

Smiling warmly, Arthur Kincaid looked at each of the guests assembled and said, "Thank you. You will all get to know each other better during our luncheon in the Royal

Ballroom. I should also tell you that I have taken the liberty of including each of your resumes in the packet of information which will be distributed to you at the end of the session. Well now, let's get started with the business at hand."

He nodded to Hartwell who promptly set the activities in motion. Butlers carrying silver trays were ushered into the Boardroom to offer coffee or tea and a delicious Portuguese pastry, fresh baked malasadas. Two additional assistants, clones of the officious Hartwell, handed out leather bound folders with each participant's name engraved on the cover.

Scott was enjoying the malasadas which tasted like his Mom's special sugar dumplings and had just started a conversation with Makiko from Japan when Hartwell reappeared. Following him was a large contingent of security guards carrying an antique treasure chest with padlocks on both hasps and further secured by thick leather straps. The chest was placed on a table in the back of the room where Hartwell made a visible display of producing two separate skeleton keys which opened the heavy brass padlocks. Two of the guards wearing white gloves carefully removed a rectangular, transparent box made of glass which contained a manuscript bound on both sides by 1/2 inch thick koa wood panels. The wood was finely polished and hinged by wide gold clasps inlaid with rubies. The front of the cover was embossed with an intricate gold leaf design. The box was placed in the center of the oak conference table directly in front of Scott's seat. Arthur Kincaid stepped forward saying, "It gives me great pleasure to introduce to you Dr. Gregory Rosenquist from the Institute of Scientific National Research in Utah. Dr. Rosenquist earned his Ph.D at the University of Cambridge and taught at the University of Bristol before assuming his current position at Utah. Dr. Rosenquist."

Scott, clapping politely along with the rest of the group, wondered if he could keep his curiosity in check for much longer. He had met Rosenquist at an archaeological conference just last year and knew his background as an expert in the carbon-14 dating process. Rosenquist had studied under Professor Williard Libby, the American inventor of the carbo-14 clock, the geiger counter instrument for which he won the 1960 Nobel prize in chemistry.

"Mr. Kincaid has asked me here today," Rosenquist began, speaking in his clipped German accent, "to authenticate the age of the bound parchment you see before you. I am pleased to confirm that using the most up to date radiocarbon dating instruments available, the tests place the date of the manuscript anywhere between the period 30 A.D. to 60 A.D."

For just a minute, a hushed silence fell over the room as each of the guests digested the significance of Rosenquist's statement and mulled over the more important questions. What was the content of the manuscript? Who wrote it? All at once the questions poured out.

Roberto DiMartino was the first to call out, "Is it a Biblical text?

Irena chimed in, "Tell us, is it about Augustus Caesar, the Emperor?"

Nancy drawled, "This is important, isn't it?

Holding his hands up to quiet the group Arthur Kincaid nodded his head approvingly while escorting his next resident expert up to the podium.

"I appreciate your enthusiasm. I assure you that all your

questions will soon be answered. For now, let me introduce you to Professor Nina Carbonelle, an expert linguist who specializes in Hebrew, Greek and Aramaic and is highly praised for her part in the translation of the Dead Sea Scrolls. She currently holds the Principal Chair of Kingston College in London. Professor, you have the floor."

Quickly stepping up to the mike, the attractive young woman with hypnotic almond eyes held everyone's attention.

"Thank you, Mr. Kincaid," she began, "for giving me the opportunity to work on this project with my new found colleagues. I never dreamed that while on sabbatical I would be able to do research on such a fascinating topic. I, too, can confirm after scrupulously examining the text contained in this unique manuscript, that it is authentic."

Dr. Howard Stassen was the next expert introduced. With a doctorate from Oxford, England, his research and publication list was highly impressive. Surprisingly, the short, powerfully built Doctor did not fit the image of the dry scientist. He punctuated his brief comments with hand gestures, clearly unable to conceal in his pale blue eyes his fresh enthusiasm for this project.

"I have carefully examined the ink used in writing the manuscript contained in this booklet. I put it through every test, using every modern technology available. I had my staff conduct extensive research using our computer banks and have come to the same conclusion as my colleagues. This booklet dates to the early first century of our Lord, 30 A.D. to 60 A.D."

Arthur Kincaid stood confidently next to Stassen, asking the group to acknowledge him with their applause. "Our deepest appreciation to you, Dr. Stassen, and also to your esteemed colleagues, Dr. Rosenquist and Professor Carbonelle, for sharing your convictions with our guests this morning.

Suddenly all eyes turned to Hartwell who was accompanied by one of his cloned assistants carefully holding an intricately carved staff approximately six feet in length. Hartwell motioned to him to place it in the middle of the antique oak conference table.

"Please feel free to look more closely at this staff, ladies and gentlemen," exclaimed Arthur Kincaid. "However, since it has been in my family for almost two thousand years, I would appreciate your not picking it up without first putting on the white gloves which are available from Mr. Hartwell."

Scott was the first to don his protective gloves, anxiously ready and waiting to inspect the staff which Hartwell gingerly handed to him. Slowly reading the names from the bottom and turning the staff in a counter clockwise direction, Scott could clearly make out the names hand carved in the staff...Arthur Kincaid III 1967…Arthur Kincaid II 1932...Arthur Kincaid I 1897…Theodore Kakalouros 1862…Alexander Kakalouros II 1827…Alexander Kakalouros I 1792…

It was obvious to Scott that this was indeed a genealogy staff. The names were carved in sequence for each generation. He continued scanning the names which were now written in Greek easily making out the names until the year 742 A.D.…

The names from the year 707 changed to Aramaic until Anno Domini 322, then back to Greek. The carvings became more difficult to decipher but Scott pressed on urgently, determined to solve the mystery of the generations.

Nearing the top of the staff, Scott identified the names for the years 147 and 112 as Hebrew. Finally he reached the last inscription but he could not make out the last name carved in letters. Looking up to Kincaid for help, Scott exclaimed, "This is unbelievable," not realizing he was speaking out loud.

Arthur Kincaid III proclaimed, "Yes, it's true, Professor Hamilton, my lineage which you have been tracing on our family staff goes back to the year 77 A.D. Our family tree begins with our oldest known ancestor. His name was 'Melchior', one of the Three Wise Men, the Magi mentioned in the Bible."

Chapter Three:

The Magi

"Melchior, our beloved ancestor, was indeed a wise man," continued Arthur Kincaid, pausing briefly to let his guests recover from their initial shock. "As a seeker of knowledge, he traveled the world extensively, writing about the wonders he encountered. This bound manuscript which you see before you contains his memoirs but most importantly it also contains his last wish and testament."

Looking around the conference table to gauge their reactions, Arthur Kincaid pressed on, "Every generation of our family," he said emphatically, "has honored Melchior's final request. From our forefathers who controlled the caravan routes from Arabia to Greece; to our family tribes who dominated the shipping industry throughout the Mediterranean in the Middle Ages; from the immigrants who joined the rush to a brave new world called America in the 16th century; to the descendants who helped establish the 13 colonies; up to the generation of my grandfather, Arthur Kincaid III. Today, I follow in the footsteps of my father and his father before him as we have done every twenty five years since the year 77 A.D."

The hush of silence was deafening. No one wanted to break the trance which Arthur Kincaid had cast with his magical tale. It seemed to be a story straight out of the "Arabian Nights."

"Our mission," Arthur Kincaid explained, "is to continue the Dream of Melchior. We spend a considerable amount of time qualifying a select group of people such as the gathering here today. The first symposium I took part in was the year 1967. The guests invited were from Australia, Singapore, Hungary, Greece, Libya, Switzerland, Chicago and Hawaii from the United States, Ethiopia, Turkey, Canada, Brazil, Mexico and Ireland. As you can see, one of the requirements of our task is to ensure a global reach. In 1967, as a 10 year old boy I was expected to begin my training in the family business. And above all things in my education, my father made sure I understood the importance of our Symposium."

Taking a deep breath, Arthur Kincaid continued, "Today I am going to ask all of you to make a commitment to keep an open mind." On cue, Hartwell and his assistants distributed brand new brown leather briefcases to each guest around the table. "You will find in your briefcase a translation of Melchior's memoirs. I ask that you spend the weekend reading his story and share it with your spouse. Once you have read this 2000 year old diary, you will understand why we have invited you to our symposium. Right now you will have an opportunity to get to know one another better over lunch. Your afternoon is free. Tonight you are all invited to attend a barbecue dinner given in your honor in Central Park. When you return to your room, you will find your briefcase with further instructions and your copy of the Memoirs waiting for you. Tomorrow, please return here to the boardroom at 6:00 P.M. We will find out if you are willing to take up the task."

After Arthur Kincaid's closing remarks, the group gathered in the Royal Ballroom for an extravagant buffet which featured the Waldorf's signature dishes: Penne Pasta with Chicken Tenderloin served with roasted peppers and veal glaze along with Sautéed Pork Tenderloin and Rosemary Potato accompanied by a homemade mozzarella relish.

Scott could barely hear the whispered conversations as they

went through the buffet line but he knew the talk centered on one topic - Melchior's diary and what impact it might have on the world's knowledge of the first century A.D. - of the Baby Jesus and the birth of Christianity.

Not wishing to be rude, Scott engaged in polite banter with Chao Lin Dang who was seated to his left and with William MacCary on his right. Chao was a successful direct marketing executive specializing in cosmetics; MacCary, a barrister based in the center of London. As the resident archaeologist, Scott was bombarded with their questions.

"Have you heard of the existence of this diary before, Professor?" Chao probed.

Before Scott could respond, MacCary interrupted as attorneys are wont to do, "I know Kincaid provided expert witnesses to authenticate the manuscript, but my question is why has this been kept a secret for so long? What do you think, Hamilton?"

Chao insistent, asked, "Do you believe it really is a diary of one of the Magi, Professor Hamilton?"

Struggling to keep his own emotions from erupting, Scott put on his best professional demeanor and firmly stated, "I have no reason to doubt the veracity of the scholars who certified the manuscript as dating from the first century. However, I think it best not to jump to any conclusions until we have read the diary first hand, don't you?" Eavesdropping on the conversation, Gustav Kreiger, an automobile and insurance salesman in Germany, stopped by the table to join in the discussion.

"Professor, I heard that you agree with the specialists we heard today. I know the story of the three Magi bringing gifts to the baby Jesus, but where did they come from, who were they?"

A crowd was quickly gathering around Scott now to listen to his answer, including Omar, Wilma, Martin and Roberto. Cesar Ruiz, a reporter for the daily "Morning Star" newspaper in Madrid, enthusiastically jumped in, "I bet that Sister Carol knows the answer to that." All eyes turned to the smiling nun, dressed in the traditional white habit of her religious order, the Sisters of the Sacred Hearts.

Scott, grateful to have the attention diverted away from himself, shook his head in agreement with Cesar and said, "Yes, go ahead, Sister, tell us about the Magi."

Sister Carol, not needing any further encouragement, began with relish, recounting the story she must have told hundreds of times before to the children in her orphanage.

"Tradition tells us that the Three Kings of the Orient, or Magi, followed the Star of Bethlehem to Israel to pay homage to the new born Christ Child. Each of the pilgrims brought gifts with them. Melchior came bearing gold, Balthazar brought frankincense and Gaspar offered as his gift the precious ointment, myrrh. These gifts are believed to be the symbols for Faith, Hope and Charity."

While Nancy, Makiko, Franz Robelle and Irena moved in closer to hear more clearly, Sister Carol reached into her large handbag and pulled out a small, obviously worn copy of the Jerusalem Bible. "Let's look at the original version of the story from Mathew's Gospel," she said proudly and began to read from Chapter 2 verses 1-23:

"Now Jesus having been born in Bethlehem of Judea in the days of Herod the King, behold, Magi, from the east, arrived in Jerusalem saying; "Where is the one born King of the Jews? We saw his star at its rising, and came to worship him." Now hearing this, King Herod was troubled and all the inhabitants of Jerusalem with him.

Having assembled all the chief priest and the scribes of the people, he inquired from them where the Christ was to be born. They told him, in Bethlehem of Judea, for it has been written through the prophet; 'And you Bethlehem in the land of Judah, among the rulers of Judah, are not at all the least. For out of you will come forth a ruler of Judah who will shepherd my people-Israel.' Then Herod, secretly calling the Magi, inquired carefully from them the time of the appearing star. Sending them to Bethlehem he said: 'Go and question carefully concerning the child, and when you find him report to me so that I also may come and worship him. 'So hearing the king they went."

Pausing for effect, Sister Carol's eyes grew bigger and with a dramatic flair she finished the biblical account without having to look at the text, "Behold! The star that they had seen at its rising in the east went before them until coming, it stood over where the child was. Seeing the star they rejoiced with an exceeding great joy. Coming into the house they saw the child with Mary, his mother. Falling down they worshiped him and opening their treasures they offered him gifts; gold, frankincense and myrrh. Having been warned by a dream not to return to Herod, they departed by another way to their own country."

Omar, a doctor at Mount Sinai's major hospital, asked inquiringly, "Is that the only version of the gospels which mentions the Magi?"

"Yes, it is, Omar," replied Sister Carol.

"Then where do we get the names Melchior, Balthazar and Gaspar?" Omar interjected.

Irena, who was a gymnastics and fitness instructor and looked the part with her slim, athletic build, quickly added, "What about the fact that nowhere in Matthew's telling of the story is there any mention about how many Magi there were. Why three? And Matthew does not refer to them as Kings?"

Franz Robelle, the head concierge of Paris' five Star Hotel 'Le Sofitel' added, "What about the camels? Matthew doesn't mention their mode of transportation?"

Wilma Ortal, a first grade teacher from Manilla, raised her hand and at the same time spoke hurriedly so she could get her question in, "I remember, as a child, seeing on the stain glass window of the church we attended the images of the Three Kings: one was Asian, another European, the third African. Is this true?"

Nancy Demary, a housewife and part time realtor offered, "Maybe political correctness existed even before the 1990's do ya' suppose?"

Gustav jumped in again, "That's exactly the question I asked earlier. If we can figure out where they came from, we'd have a better idea who they were."

Martin Steinberg, a successful banker from Jerusalem, fidgeted with his tie, looking extremely uncomfortable during this exchange. He kept his gaze lowered so no one could catch his attention and try to get him involved in the conversation.

"Whoa, Whoa!" exclaimed Roberto, Rome's favorite high school soccer coach accustomed to shouting above the crowd. "Lets give the Sister a break here."

Thank you, Roberto, I appreciate your concern," Sister Carol answered, "but I assure you that my children back home in our orphanage are much more demanding. I will answer as many of the questions I can and then depend on Professor Hamilton to fill in the rest."

"I have a problem, Sister," Numi Tafasau's voice

boomed from the back of the room. The six foot six former professional football player turned social worker for his island home of Tahiti was an imposing figure as he stood stretched out to his full height, waving his hands to get her attention.

"When did the Magi arrive, bringing their gifts? Was it right after Jesus' birth, the same time as the shepherds? If so, then why does Matthew say 'house' and not 'stable?'"

Cesar, assuming his reporter's role, cut in, "Yes, it's always been a pet peeve of mine, about the actual date of the birth of baby Jesus. We always assumed it was 1 A.D. I mean, isn't that what the A.D. stands for - anno domini - 'in the year of our Lord'? Now some scholars say it was really 4 B.C. or 4 A.D. or even as late as 7 A.D."

Before Cesar could catch his breath, Nancy found her opening, "What about the star? Did everyone see it or just the Magi? How long were they following it?"

Martin Steinberg, caught up in the flow, jumped up and blurted out unexpectedly, "Why is Christmas celebrated on December 25th?" Catching himself for thinking out loud, he sheepishly slipped back down in his chair to the roar of good natured laughter all around.

William MacCary, loosening his tie, complimented his new found colleagues, "I dare say, you would all make good prosecuting attorneys for the London Bar."

The laughter continued as everyone settled in and looked to Sister Carol to continue with her explanation.

Hartwell entered the Presidential Suite on the penthouse floor of the Waldorf-Astoria. He found Arthur Kincaid in the living room studying a portfolio of ancient maps spread out on a large oak table. Peering up from his granny glasses which he usually wore while examining the old manuscripts from his personal library, he excitedly beckoned Hartwell to join him.

"Come in, Keith. Here, look at this. Can you make this out? Is this a beta or delta?" Hartwell, fluent in several languages including ancient Greek, picked up the magnifying glass from the conference table and scanned the Greek letters in question.

"Definitely a delta in my opinion."

"Exactly what I was thinking," replied Arthur.

Both men smiled.

Adjourning to the open deck overlooking the Hudson River and the Statue of Liberty for a cup of tea, Hartwell recounted every detail of the discussion going on in the Royal Ballroom including Martin Steinberg's surprise outburst.

"Everything is going well according to your plan. Your father would have been proud of you, Arthur." Hartwell stood looking down at the young man for whom he had served as mentor since Arthur Kincaid the II had died twenty years ago.

"Thank you, Keith. We shall see what kind of impact the class of Symposium 2002 has on the world."

Chapter Four:

Myth or Fact

Sister Carol began anew with even more enthusiasm than before with an attentive, appreciative audience. "Even though the biblical account is not as specific, oral tradition and depictions in art such as paintings and mosaics have provided details with were of great interest to the early Christians. Drawings from the roman catacombs sometimes depict only two Magi presenting gifts to the child, sometimes four but there are other examples of medieval art which show as many as twelve Wise Men. Most often, however, we find three Wise Men, one for each of the three gifts: gold, frankincense and myrrh.

Different names were given to the Magi through the years maybe because of transliteration difficulties in the various languages and inconsistency in the spelling. In any case, the most commonly accepted names in the Western tradition are the three names I mentioned before: Melchior, Balthazar and Gaspar. By the early middle ages, it was already firmly established that they represented three different races, not, I believe for any political reasons but more than likely because they came from different parts of the world. Their races, their ages and their images were quite often interchanged. So Melchior sometimes is described as an old Hindu man with a long beard, sometimes as a young, beardless, white European."

Walking back and forth in front of the group, Sister Carol paused for a second then continued, "Let's see, that should take care of your question, Omar, about the Magi's names. Irena, you asked why the number of three so I hope I've given you a satisfactory explanation. Now as to where the idea came from that the Magi were Kings I'll find that in the Old Testament."

Paging through her well thumbed book, the fresh faced nun was obviously enjoying the exercise. "O.K., here it is! From Psalms 68:29, 'Because of your temple at Jerusalem, kings will bring you gifts.' Also, from Psalms 72:10 'The kings of Tarshish and of distant shores will bring tribute to him; the kings of Sheba and Seba will present him gifts.' End of quote."

Not waiting for any comments, Sister Carol pressed on. "As for your question, Makiko, since camels were regularly used in this part of the world for caravans, it was not far fetched for the early Christians to accept the image of the three Magi riding these creatures on their journey which was probably a long one. As to the questions where did they come from and when did they arrive, we'll turn that over to the Professor."

Sister Carol sat down to any outpouring of applause from the group which she acknowledged by standing for an encore and making a quick curtsy.

"Come on, Professor," Roberto beckoned, "tell us what you know about where the Magi came from."

A shy person by nature when speaking one on one, Scott's personality blossomed in front of an audience, so without any further urging he took his place in front of the group and launched into his lecture.

"The Bible does not mention whether the Magi all came from the same country or journeyed independently and met up somewhere following the star. Most scholars will agree, however, that the major possibilities for their country of origin are the following. The first is Arabia. Early Christian writers such as Clement of Rome in his letter to the Corinthians mentions frankincense and myrrh from places near 'Arabia.' Also if my memory serves me right, Justin around 150 A.D. specifically wrote in his Dialogue, 'Magi from Arabia came to him,' i.e. King Herod."

Scott hesitated for a second, tapping his right temple with his forefinger, a habit he picked up when trying to emphasize a point, then quickly approached Sister Carol.

"Something Sister said a few minutes ago reminded me of another biblical quote. Sister, may I borrow your Bible, please?"

Quickly paging through the Old Testament, Scott excitedly said, "Yes, here it is, Psalm 72:15, 'Long may he live! May gold from Sheba be given to him. May people ever pray for him and bless him all day long.'

And here's another Old Testament passage which supports Arabia as a strong possibility as our source. In Isaiah 60:6 it says, 'Herds of camels will cover your land, young camels of Midian and Epah. And all from Sheba will come bearing gold and incense and proclaiming the praise of the Lord.' End quote."

Omar nodding in agreement, spoke up, "And Sheba is in the south-western part of Arabia."

"That's correct, Omar."

"Wasn't there an ancient temple unearthed there not too long ago, Professor?", asked Martin now becoming engaged in the discussion.

"Yes, as a matter of fact, one of my students participated in that archaeological dig at Marib, which was once the capital of Sheba. Artifacts clearly establish that the temple dates as far back as the 7th century B.C. and was dedicated to a moon-goddess, Ilumquh. All indications are that the people of Sheba were ruled by Kings and Priests who worshiped the sun and the moon.

Also, the 'people of the east' were often associated with wisdom as in this passage from 1 Kings 4:30."

Scott read from Sister Carol's Bible, "Solomon's wisdom was greater that the wisdom of all the men of the East, and greater than all the wisdom of Egypt."

"You convinced me, Professor," exclaimed Numi in his deep baritone voice. "It must have been Arabia. That's why they were all riding camels." Nancy, Makiko and Roberto in a gesture of support gave Numi the thumbs up sign.

MacCary interrupted, "Just a minute. Let's hear all the possibilities before we make any unwarranted assumptions. The Professor said there were several options."

Smiling, Scott thought about what a wonderful feeling it was to have such a captive audience. How could he get his young college students as interested in his lectures as these baby boomers? Or was that just wishful thinking?

"Isn't that right, Professor?" MacCary asked.

"Yes, William. There are two other major possibilities, Persia for one. Certainly many people in the early Christian Church assumed so. There is a legend based on medieval writings that about 600 A.D. the Persian armies invaded the Holy Land destroying villages and churches. According to the story, when the armies approached the Basilica of Bethlehem, they ignored the orders of their commander, turned and marched onward sparing the church and the town."

Not able to contain her curiosity, Chao blurted out, "But why?"

"Because they saw a mosaic through the Church

window with the images of the Magi offering gifts to Mary and the Child. The Magi were dressed in belted tunics wearing Phrygian caps. The armies recognized them as Persians."

Looking around at the faces before him, Scott could see a seed of doubt creeping in about their decision just a few minutes before that Arabia was the home country of the Magi.

He added, "One other thing that convinced Clement of Alexandria, one of the Church Fathers, is the evidence in Persian writings about the coming of the Messiah. I can't guarantee a word for word quote but if memory serves me well, the apocryphal Arabic Gospel talks about the Magi 'coming to Jerusalem according to the prediction of Zoroaster.' Zoroastrianism is the philosophy of its Persian founder. It is conjecture that the Magi knew about this pagan prophecy and perhaps others."

Deciding to lighten things up with a little audience participation, Scott asked, "So how many of you think that the Magi came from Persia?"

Seven hands went up.

"How many of you think that Arabia is the correct answer?"

Three hands were raised quickly, then hesitantly three more people watching what the others were doing slowly joined in.

"O.K. that leaves only Irena, William and Martin without any commitment."

Playfully acting the part, MacCary the barrister stood up and intoned, "Your Honor, I believe I speak for the three of us. We respectfully stand by our right to reserve our opinion until all the evidence is in, thank you!"

MacCary sat back down to a chorus of hissing and booing led by Roberto and Numi.

Hartwell, standing behind the dessert table in the back of the room, watched the goings on with gratification. His thoughts turned to the many potential candidates that were on the select list for review but were not invited. He had made his recommendations but Arthur made the final decision to invite only those in the ballroom. He had made the right decision. These were people who had never met one another twenty four hours before and yet they were interacting in a way which was beyond expectation. His years of experience dealing with different personalities convinced him that these were indeed special individuals.

Holding up both his arms to quiet the group after MacCary's impromptu monologue Scott got back on track.

"The final prospect for the home base of the Magi is Babylon. The evidence suggests that they were the foremost astronomers in the ancient world and left extensive records of their discoveries and inventions. Also, add to this the fact that many Jews remained in Babylon after the Exile in 6th Century B.C. so the Jewish Messianic prophesies would have been well known to the Magi."

Paging through Sister Carol's Bible once again, Scott began reading, "This passage is from Daniel 1:20 regarding Daniel's interpretation of the Dream of King Nabuchodonosor, King of Babylon: 'And in all matters of wisdom and understanding that the king inquired of them he found them ten times better than all the diviners and wise men that were in all his kingdom.'

The early Christian writers don't mention Babylon at the top of the list, but many modern scholars are convinced that the Magi were Babylonian."

Gustav immediately turned to MacCary and insisted that he make a decision.

"You've got all the information now, Mac. What's your pick? Arabia, Persia or Babylon?"

Irena interjected, "Don't presume to speak for me, Mr. Mac. I am thinking now that the correct origin is Persia."

Not wanting to be left out of the loop, Martin quickly challenged MacCary in turn. "I also choose to represent myself Pro Se. I opt to take the Fifth."

Rising slowly to his feet, William straightened his tie and buttoned his jacket while walking to the front of the room. Clearing his throat, he began in his pompous way, "All right. Let's summarize the situation. There are seven votes for Persia, six for Arabia, one abstention and the Professor gets no vote and has to recuse himself. I assume that the overriding factor which swayed the majority of you to opt for Persia was your emotional reaction to the legend of the Basilica of Bethlehem. Discounting that and the fact that the rest of you picked Arabia because you were influenced by our good minister, Numi's comment about the camels, I do not need to analyze the evidence any further. The rule of contrariness demands that my vote be cast for Babylon.

After the laughter died down, Cesar and Wilma spoke up at the same time, "Professor!" Uncharacteristically for a reporter, Cesar, quite the gentleman, apologized and prompted Wilma to go first.

"Thank you, Cesar," Wilma began. "Professor, I was just going to ask you to continue your discussion about the time line - what year was the Baby Jesus born? And when did the Star which the Magi followed appear?"

Before Scott could answer, several waiters appeared carrying refreshments in 9" tall glasses filled to the top with crushed ice. Grateful for the intermission to gather his thoughts, Scott was surprised when in less than a minute every single one of the group had grabbed a drink, sat back down and appeared eager to hear his reply.

Taking a sip of his Coca Cola, and removing his wool sport coat with leather patches on the elbows, Scott clapped his hands together and declared, "All right! You asked for it," shaking his finger at everyone as was his habit when he got down and serious.

"FYI, the calendar has been one of the most controversial factors for division in the Christian Church. I'm sure you don't want a full dissertation on this topic which could take a whole semester so I am going to cover this as simply and succinctly as possible. And, for our purposes we will concentrate on Christmas and the Magi. Let's begin with some basic definitions.

A.U.C. stands for the Latin 'ab urbe condita' which translated means 'from the founding of the city.' i.e. Rome.

B.C. means 'Before Christ and A.D. equals the Latin 'in anno Domini' translated 'in the year of our Lord.' as Cesar mentioned previously. Remember that in the B.C./A.D. formula, there is no year zero. So keep in mind that after 31 December 1 B.C. came A.D. 1 January 1.

The use of the A.D. dating system did not occur until late in the Middle ages and extensive use of the B.C. dating system did not take place until the late 17th century. Of course, it's understandable that the ancient Romans, from whom we derive many of our western traditions, e.g. the calendar, did not view their existence as being in the B.C. ('before Christ') period. On the contrary, most ancient civilizations did not count the years from a specified starting point but rather used the regnal system such as 'in the fourteenth year of the reign of Julius Caesar' or 753 A.U.C. ('753 years from the founding of Rome')."

Omar stood up and asked, "Professor, how in the world can anyone reconcile the differences in the dating systems world wide? Just as an example, from my own personal background in the Coptic Church, originally from the ancient Egyptian tradition, our New Year is celebrated on September 11. And I believe the Chinese celebrate their New Year in February."

As soon as Omar stopped speaking, Chao cheerfully offered, "Everybody invited to nine course Chinese dinner at my uncle's "Chinese Phoinix" restaurant in China town to celebrate 'Year of the Horse' on February 12."

"I accept," responded Roberto, followed by a chorus of 'Count me in' and 'Me, too,' from some of the others.

"Thank you, Omar for your input and since I'm always looking for an excuse to get back to the Big Apple, you can plan on my being at your New Year's party, Chao. "To answer your question, Omar, Scott continued, "there are various calendars such as the ones you mentioned, the Coptic and Ethiopian and the Chinese. There's also the Soviet Calendar, the Japanese Calendar, the French Revolutionary Calendar, the Islamic Calendar, the Hindu Calendar, the Persian Calendar and I'm sure others of which I'm not familiar."

"No wonder you can't get a straight answer when you ask a woman her age," Franz Robelle interjected. "She can always claim she was born under a different calendar."
Stopping short after noticing the icy stares from Irena and Makiko, Franz raised both his arms in mock defense and offered a shallow apology.

"Don't mind the Frenchman, Professor," added Sister Carol, "please fill us in on the rest of the story."

"For our purposes, let's concentrate on the Julian Calendar. Do you recall my mentioning Julius Caesar? Well, in the year 46 B.C., one of Julius' responsibilities as the 'Pontifex Maximus' (the high priest) was to straighten out the mess in the calendar. I need to advise you that there are various theories on the details but to keep matters simple, here's what Julius supposedly did.

Abandoning the formula for a calendar based on the lunar cycles, he moved the start of the year from March 1 to January 1 which is now our New Year. In order to restructure the old calendar, Julius realized he needed to increase the existing 355 day calendar year. To begin with, he extended the year 46 B.C. to 455 days (annus confusionis 'year of confusion') as a one time adjustment, introduced the concept of 'leap year' every four years and from 45 B.C. on he added ten additional days to a year, eleven in leap years. Spreading out the increase over the months, Julius added two days to January, August and December, one day each to the months of April, June, September and November."

"Professor, I had to take Latin as a requirement in high school," Wilma interjected, "and it always confused me knowing that the months of September, October, November and December are misnomers for the seventh, eighth, ninth and tenth months of the year."

"You're absolutely correct, Wilma," Scott replied, "when March was the beginning of the year, it made sense. I assume that all the names of the months based on numbers would have eventually been changed such as January so called in honor of the god Janus with two faces, one looking to the past of the old year, the other to the future of the new year."

In jest Scott quipped, "Maybe Cleopatra, and I don't mean Miss Taylor, kept Julius so busy he didn't have the energy to complete the calendar reform he started. In any case, after the Ides of March in 44 B.C., the date of Caesar's assassination, he literally ran out of time. His adopted son and successor, Octavian, assumed the name of Augustus

Caesar which means "revered" and assigned this name to the month following July so called in memory of Julius Caesar."

"I wish our Latin teacher, Sister Laurentia, would have taught us more about the history and not dwelt on things like the conjugation of verbs 'amo, amas, amat, amamus, amatis, amant," Wilma recited.

"That nun was so strict if she caught us chewing gum she'd make us stick it on our nose and keep it there for the whole class. She…oh, sorry, Sister Carol." Realizing her dilemma, Wilma stopped in mid sentence, "I didn't mean…"

"No offense taken, Wilma," Sister Carol assured her.

Irena, taking advantage of the pregnant pause, spoke up, "So Professor, you're just preparing us for more confusion on the actual date of Christmas, aren't you?"

Caught with what Ellen referred to as his "Cheshire Cat" mischievous smile, Scott admitted, "You got me, Irena. Sad to say, I can't give you any definitive answers. Just like the origin of the Magi, I can only present the prevailing theories and you'll have to make your own decision."

Taking a deep breath, Scott renewed his presentation,. "Let me introduce you to a medieval monk called Dionysius Exiguus. Around the middle of the 5th century A.D., Dionysius, a renowned scholar of Church records was asked by Pope John I to help solve all the dissension about when Easter should be celebrated. We won't go down that road right now, but suffice it to say, Dionysius also calculated the dates for the Nativity. Dionysius proposed that the 'Annunciation' (i.e. the Angel appearing to Mary) occurred on March 25, 753 A.U.C. or as we moderns refer to it 1 B.C. the nativity is assigned the date December 25, 753 A.U.C. or 1 B.C.

Cesar, sensing an inconsistency, blurted out loud, 'Professor, I thought that the Nativity was supposed to be 1 A.D.?"

"I think it will be clearer when we add to the Annunciation and Nativity the Feast of the Circumcision, Cesar. Some cultures count the beginning of a person's life from birth, others will go back to the date of conception. In the Orthodox Jewish tradition, life does not officially begin until the boy is named and circumcised."

Sister Carol already anticipating Scott's reference, began to read from her ever present compendium, 'And when eight days were accomplished for the circumcising of the child, his name was called Jesus...' "this passage is from Luke 2:21."

"Thank you, Sister Carol." Scott looked at Cesar and holding up his right hand started counting on his fingers.

"I get it, Professor. Eight days from December 25 B.C. 1 takes us into January 1 A.D. 1 because as you laid it out before, there's no zero year."

"That's an A+ Cesar," beamed Scott.

Hartwell caught a glimpse of the attractive blonde strolling past the large picture window of the Waldorf's front entrance with the Goldens in tow. She had on Calvin Klein blue jeans, a thick yellow ski sweater and moon boots. She was obviously in trouble, balancing packages of presents in both arms and trying to hold onto the two retrievers - one, a male with a huge St. Bernard head weighing well over a hundred pounds, the other a frisky female with a mind of her own. Rushing out to lend a hand, Hartwell couldn't help but chide her.

"Mrs. Kincaid, I told you we would have the staff get the presents for the guests."

Taking off her sunglasses and revealing her hazel green eyes, Karen Kincaid smiled, planted a kiss on Hartwell's cheek and dashed down the hallway calling "Come Buster, Come Goldie."

Scott looked at his watch. Years of experience giving fifty minute lectures to his college classes had set off his automatic timer.

"All right, Ladies & Gentelemen, before you all fall asleep on me, we'll have to finish our discussion on the 'Star of Bethlehem.'"

MacCary, imitating the attorney declared incompetent for falling asleep during a trial which the O'Reilly Factor just featured on prime time, stood up slurring his words, "I object, Hamilton!"

The athletic Irena, in one swift motion, grabbed MacCary by the scruff of his neck, forced him back down in his seat and stuffed a napkin into his mouth to the howls of delight from the cheering crowd.

"Don't worry, Professor, he won't interrupt you again."

"Bravo, Irena. You'll be the envy of every anti-lawyer crusade in the country."

After the laughter died down, Scott began, "We don't have a blackboard, so you'll have to remember the names and theories proposed. there will be an oral quiz after we review the material."

Groans from Roberto, Franz and Gustav.

"Johannes Kepler in 1604 lent his support to the idea that the Star of Bethlehem could have been a supernova. The scientific details on how or what produces a supernova escapes me. Physics was not my favorite subject, but what I do know is that when a star's core runs out of nuclear power and it starts to decay, rather than dissipating slowly it explodes into a brilliant burst of light. Supernovas are such spectacular events they can even be seen during the day and their lingering brightness can last for several months. Astronomers argue that the frequency of supernovas in the Milky Way galaxy is a random occurrence perhaps no more that once every few hundreds of years.

Another theory put forth by Kepler is the conjunction of the planets Jupiter, Saturn and Mars which also occurred in 1604. He knew that Jewish tradition focused on such planetary conjunctions and that astronomical computations predict that this specific occurrence happened every 805 years. Babylonian and Chinese records from that period of time confirm these calculations. Kepler then proposed that these 'meeting of the planets' foretold momentous events in history, a harbinger of great things if you will. His examples included Charlemagne in 800 A.D.; Jesus in 5 B.C.; Isaiah in 810 B.C. and Moses in 1610 B.C. Note that using this formula, Christmas is five or so years off from our friend Dionysius' calendar.

The last plausible theory is that the Star of Bethlehem was in fact a comet and not a star. Sister Carol, would you mind reading that passage from Matthew so we can hear the specific language about the star?'

Sister Carol finding the reference in a heartbeat, read "…'and behold the star which they had seen in the east went before them until it came and stood over where the child was. And seeing the star they rejoiced with exceeding great joy.' This is from Matthew 2: 9-10."

"Once again, we appreciate your help, Sister. Now, analyzing that passage, what conclusions can we draw?"

"It was a moving star!" Chao proudly contributed.

Omar exclaimed, "The star reappeared after not being

visible for awhile. That's why the Magi were so happy. they thought they had lost their guiding light."

Numi added, "But why does it say 'stood over', Professor?"

Scott responded, "The ancients characteristically identified comets as portents of great events such as the birth and death of kings. The Roman historian Dion Cassius described the comet of 12 B.C. as 'standing for several days over the city.' By the way, I'm sure you all know the name of this famous comet of 12 B.C."

Martin volunteered, "Halley's comet."

"Good job, Martin," echoed Roberto and Sister Carol.

"Could Halley's comet be the Star of Bethlehem, Professor?" asked Makiko.

Scott replied, "Halley's comet is as dependable as Old Faithful in Yellowstone Park. It reappears every seventy six years right on schedule. The last time this famous celestial body passed our way was in 1986 and we can count on it coming again in 2062.

But to answer your question, Makiko, 12 B.C. is probably too early to fit into our paradigm. If the Star of Bethlehem was a comet, it was probably the one which passed through around 5 B.C. which was also documented in the Chinese historical records of the period.

Taking into consideration the fact that many scholars since the Middle Ages believe that Dionysius was off by four years for establishing the date of the Nativity, the comet of 5 B.C. fits right into that revised pattern. The argument supporting the idea that Dionysius was in error is that he misinterpreted Clement of Alexandria's statement that Jesus was born in the twenty-eighth year of the reign of Augustus. Dionysius assumes that Clement meant 28 B.C. when Octavian was officially given the name of Augustus by the Roman Senate. More than likely, however, Clement was actually referring to 31 B.C., the date when Octavian defeated Antony and Cleopatra at the battle of Actium. This would have made more of an impression on Clement or anyone living in Alexandria, the seat of the Nile at that time."

"So Professor, since Mac wouldn't let you vote in our last election, why don't you give us a hint?" Cesar asked. "What theory do you believe is the most plausible? What was the Star of Bethlehem?"

Roberto, supporting Cesar, jumped up and shouted, "All in favor of the Professor exposing himself, raise your hands?"

Hands went up all around, including the contrarian MacCary. It was unanimous.

Not convinced that Roberto's idiomatic English went unnoticed since even Sister Carol seemed to be blushing, Scott launched forward with his personal opinion.

"These are our options: A. Supernova; B. Planetary Conjunction; C. Comet; D. All of the Above. The correct answer to this multiple choice question is D.

Imagine for a moment if you were one of our Magi…you were familiar with the messianic prophecies and as a learned astronomer you believed in astrological signs as the harbinger of great events. What would you have thought if you saw the planetary conjunctions happen three times in the year 5 B.C., and on top of that witness a supernova? Wouldn't you believe the time was at hand and set out on a journey of discovery? What if you lost sight of your guiding light as it were? Wouldn't you stop and ask for directions from the King of Judea whom you would assume would also be searching for the newborn King of the Jews? Wouldn't you be exceedingly glad if, pointed in the right direction, you saw a comet, the light you had lost, leading the way to Bethlehem?"

No one spoke. their thoughts were far away…in a different time…in a distant land…

Chapter Five:

Central Park

A picture postcard. No other way to describe the special event Arthur Kincaid had arranged. One group had left at 5:30. The second boarded limousines in front of the Waldorf at 6:00 P.M. and ten minutes later found themselves transported to the east entrance of New York's Central Park.

In front of the archway, there were eight powerful Clydesdale horses hitched to a red hay wagon covered on both sides by boughs of green pine sprinkled with red Christmas berries. Everyone eagerly climbed aboard, grabbed one of the colorful wool blankets on the bench and snuggled together for the ride.

The gentle giants proudly high stepped their way along the winding black top path to the center of the park. The driver called out their names to reassure them. "Big Ben" was the leader and he kept the team in tempo. With each step of their massive hooves, the two thousand pound ponies shook the bell tassels fastened to their harnesses around their massive chests and on top of their head dresses.

Listening to the bells ring, Nancy Demary, the ex-Miss America contestant from Atlanta as she liked to call herself, broke out in an impromptu rendition of "Jingle Bells, Jingle Bells." Everyone, caught up in the spirit, joined in singing aloud, "Jingle all the way, O! what fun it is to ride, in 'an eight horse open' sleigh."

Sister Carol Ann followed with a touching solo of "Amazing Grace" and then led the chorus in a rendition of "Adeste

Fidelis," alternating between the Latin original and the English version "O Come All Ye Faithful."

Scott, looking at the melting pot of faces around him, couldn't help but notice that all traces of idiosyncrasies of accent disappeared while singing the Latin, at one time the common international language of the scientific world. Listening to the English version, the crisp staccato of Gustav, Irena and Omar stood out distinctly from the smooth blending voices of Roberto, Numi or especially Nancy's comforting southern drawl.

"Penny for your thoughts, Sweetheart?" Ellen whispered in Scott's ear, resting her head on his right shoulder. "Thank you for sharing this weekend with me."

Before Scott could answer, Wilma stood up, shouting excitedly, "Look over there! Isn't that precious?"

Everyone turned in the direction Wilma pointed. Coming down the hill just behind them through any opening of the snow draped forest of trees were two huge golden retrievers strapped together with harnesses, pulling a tall driver wearing a hooded winter parka on cross country skis. Big Ben guided the team of Clydesdales to a stop. Pulling up alongside of the wagon, the x-skimusher flipped down his hood, revealing the officious Hartwell.

"Follow me, ladies and gentlemen. We'll take a shortcut."

Without waiting, Hartwell did any expertly executed turn, twirled an imaginary whip over his head, and in a perfectly pitched x-skimusher's voice, commanded the goldens to start back up the hill. Buster, the male with the St. Bernard head, batted his eyelashes, sat down defiantly and refused.

"All right! All right," Hartwell relented, reaching into his fanny pack for two large milk bone treats, "this is the last one. I mean it. Naughty Puppy!"

While all of this was going on, Nancy and Sister Carol Ann were giving instructions to Makiko, Irena, Cesar and Chao on how to do "Angels" in the snow as all the husbands watched in fascination.

"O.K. Sister. On the count of three. Y'all watch this now. One, two, three, GO!" Nancy shouted.

Nancy and Sister Carol who were standing face to face, simultaneously fell backwards in the deep powdered snow and began to wave their arms up and down repeatedly, creating perfectly shaped snow angels with wings.

In the meantime, hearing Nancy shout the command "GO!", Buster and Goldie took off in a dash, their thick paws churning the snow with the off balanced Hartwell trailing behind, unaccustomed to being totally out of control.

Reaching the top of the hill first, Irena and Roberto urged the rest of the group onward. "It's beautiful!," exclaimed Irena waving excitedly. The others picked up the pace trudging through the two snow paths created by Hartwell and the goldens.

The portly Omar, obviously in distress, kept slipping on an icy spot. Gustav and Chao helped push and pull him the rest of the way. Grateful for the help, Omar started to thank his colleagues but found himself caught up in the breathtaking sight stretching before them.

The panoramic view from their vantage point was spectacular. Above the skyline of New York City, the high cirrus clouds created a rainbow of colors with the golden hues of the setting sun. The Empire State Building stood tall in the forefront. To the right, the Statue of Liberty beaconed in silent pose, a welcome sight to all who dreamed of freedom.

Suddenly, Numi exclaimed, "Did you see it? Did you see it?" he repeated. "The Green Flash!"

"Yes, y'all. What was that?" Nancy beamed. "I saw it too."
Franz Dubuque joined in, "Oui, oui. The Green Flash. It
is a rare and special occurrence. Just as the sun sinks below
the horizon, the exact second it disappears, a bright green
light, like a camera flashbulb, goes off. I have known people
who search in vain for years but have never witnessed it,
myself included. This is my first time."

"Me too," said Makiko.

One by one, the group acknowledged that they had seen
the phenomenon. All except MacCary, who by his manner
made it clear that he was the only sane person on the hill.

Cesar attempted to explain the occurrence. "I read
somewhere that if the climatic conditions are just right, the
cloud cover, the temperature of the water, the angle of your
line of sight, the conjunction of water and sunlight creates
a prism which sparkles until the light changes direction.
So once the sun moves beneath the waterline, the prism
disappears too."

"Ancient legend says it is a harbinger of good
fortune,"continued Numi. "Some say it is the Sun's promise
to whomever sees this sign, that after a long night of rest, the
next day will bring a renewal, a chance for a new beginning,
a rebirth as it were. The past is wiped clean so the spirit can
soar with no chains holding it back. I have seen this before
from my homeland in Tahiti and in the Hawaiian Islands in
the Pacific. But I have never heard of it occurring over the
Atlantic Ocean."

"Well, I like Numi's version better," proclaimed Sister
Carol.

Martin interrupted, "I'm hungry, and from the aroma
that's coming from that bonfire down there I'm guessing the
barbecue is ready."

"Grab your bobsleds, everyone, and follow me," said

Arthur Kincaid appearing out of nowhere.

Scott jumped on his bobsled following Arthur's lead and streaked straight down the steep hill. Ellen, as well as most of the group, chose to weave back and forth in serpentine fashion. Carefully, holding on tight, teeth clenched, trying not to flip over, MacCary couldn't control his sled and plowed into Omar.

Omar in turn caused a chain reaction and created a pile up with Wilma, Franz, Cesar, Makiko and Chao all ending up in a snowbank.

Down at the bottom, Scott heard Roberto behind him.

"Not bad, Professor," Roberto commented.

"Thanks."

"For someone your age," continued Roberto.

Maybe it was just the pure joy of the wind in his face combined with the competitive spirit which made him an all-American wrestler at Minnesota during his undergraduate years, or maybe it was just baby boomer pride. Scott found himself throwing down the gauntlet, forcing Roberto to accept his challenge.

"Race you to the top and back."

"Agreed."

Irena and Numi volunteered to be the judges. While everyone completed their run down the hill in turn, Scott and Roberto readied themselves for the big race.

"On the count of three," shouted Irena, the seasoned competitor. "Get ready! One, two, three!" Numi yelled, "GO!"

The two contenders sprinted the first hundred feet up from the bottom of the hill. Gradually the steep incline forced Scott to slow his pace and stagger his steps to keep from slipping. It was obvious that Roberto, a hands-on soccer coach, was in better condition. He was already ten lengths ahead.

Cheering for the underdog, Nancy and Wilma joined Ellen in support.

"Come on, Scott. Show us what you got. Come on Scott. You can reach the top."

Embarrassed by his predicament, Scott glanced up as Roberto reached the peak, stood up and raised both arms up in triumph. Determined to finish the race no matter how far behind he was, Scott kept scrambling.

Roberto, with his "King of the Hill" smile, pushed off over the crest for his victory run downhill. Sitting upright in his sled rather than lying belly down, the overconfident Roberto, waving at his "fans" below, did not see the moving snow pile in front of him until it was too late. Unable to maneuver the sled quickly enough, he smashed into MacCary who had just dug himself out of the snowbank.

Meanwhile, Scott wasted no time in taking advantage of the situation. He had finally reached his goal and was cruising down the hill, waving the V sign as he skimmed past Roberto entangled with the red-faced MacCary.

The sound of the old west chuck wagon call to dinner was unmistakable. Hartwell kept clanging an iron rod against a metal triangle and yelling, "Come and get it!"

Karen Kincaid welcomed the group around the campfire after informal introductions, making sure everyone was warm and comfortable. Arthur had donned the trademark insignia of the master chef, the white floppy top hat and full length white apron tied twice around his waist. He asked Sister Carol to say the blessing.

"Our Father, we are grateful for this wonderful day and the fellowship of new friends from around the world. We ask that you continue to bestow your favor on our kind hosts Arthur and Karen and their children. We thank you for the food and the hands which prepared our supper. Give us the wisdom to follow in your footsteps."

"Amen," everyone joined in unison.

"Thank you, sister Carol," said Karen. "Please help yourselves everybody."

Omar jumped in line immediately followed by Martin and MacCary. Hartwell manned the first food station. A huge black pot hung on iron chains attached to a hook from the top of a tripod which spread out over a burning fire. Using a pint sized ladle, Hartwell scooped up steaming clam chowder into wooden bowls for each person in line, then directed them to Arthur.

Arthur stood over a six by four foot pit dug in the snow. White hot coals were covered up by beds of seaweed. Wielding two foot long prongs, Arthur scraped the steaming seaweed aside to reveal gigantic red lobsters with claws averaging six inches across.

Seeing the look on Scott's face as he salivated over the lobsters, Ellen had a flashback to an embarrassing moment during their college days at the University of Minnesota. They had driven across the state line to Wisconsin with some friends to enjoy an all-you-can-eat seafood buffet which featured lobster and shrimp. Scott had gone back again and again to the buffet line so many times, the manager of the restaurant decided to change the "all you can eat" policy immediately. Known as the "Hamilton Exception," the episode made the gossip rounds on the surrounding Big Ten campuses.

"I can assure you, Ellen," Arthur Kincaid began, looking directly into her eyes, "you do not have to be concerned about the 'Hamilton Exception' here." Smiling warmly he placed two three pound lobsters on a wooden platter for Scott.

"Don't ask," Scott said to Ellen as they marveled at the

feast prepared for them.

There was sweet potato, corn on the cob, baby back pork ribs, New York's famous all beef hot dogs, prepared in a dozen different ways; with sauerkraut, with chili, with onions, cheese, relish, you name it, you got it. There was an assortment of desserts including pumpkin chiffon, custard and black bottom pies, rum cake, chocolate pudding and the world famous Lappert's ice cream.

Cristie Kincaid, Arthur and Karen's eleven year old daughter, demonstrated to Chao and Omar the fine art of roasting marshmallows in preparation for creating her favorite delight, "smores."

Makiko decided to try her luck at ice skating and talked Martin into coming out onto the ice pond with her.

Sister Carol and Cesar were engaged in a snowball fight with MacCary as their adversary.

Roberto, in an effort to salve his wounded pride, talked Scott into picking teams for a coed Broom Ball tournament, a combination soccer-hockey game on ice. Numi was the first drafted, followed by Irena. Wilma joined Numi and Scott, Gustav teamed up with Roberto and Irena. Official broom ball shoes with built-in suction cups were provided by Hartwell along with brooms for everyone and the game ball.

Ellen was working on her masterpiece - a snowman with clamshells for buttons, a lobster claw for a nose, a u-curved hot dog for a smile and Arthur's chef hat to top it off.

Arthur and Karen strolled hand in hand around the frozen pond, Buster and Goldie on their heels. They found Hartwell near the Clydesdale team organizing the cleanup crew.

"Thank you for your help tonight, Keith. I believe our guests are ready to receive Melchior's challenge."

Chapter Six:

The Memoirs Book II.

Conversation was loud and boisterous as the group gathered in the boardroom of the Waldorf at 8:45 P.M. Irena and Roberto were still arguing about the last point Numi scored to put his team ahead 4-3 in the Broom Ball match. Chao, Gustav and Omar were teasing MacCary by reenacting the scene of his collision with Roberto on the hill. The camaraderie of the evening in the park continued unabated.

Hartwell had to raise his voice to get everyone's attention.

"Please take your assigned seats, ladies and gentlemen."

At exactly 9:00 P.M. Arthur Kincaid entered the room. He had changed from his heavy ski clothing to a comfortable pullover sweater, brown corduroys and loafers. The stark difference in dress and demeanor from his initial meeting with them was intentional. At 9:00 A.M. Saturday, they were guests of the Kincaid Foundation but still strangers. Tonight, twelve hours later, they were friends.

"I am sure your cup of curiosity is overflowing so I will not keep you long. I thank you for your patience and also for your cooperation. You will find in your briefcases, a letter of agreement which is self explanatory along with a translation of Melchior's Memoirs into English which was made over two hundred and fifty years ago. For the most part we have tried to stay true to the language of the original and have made few additions. The diary speaks for itself so I need not offer any further explanations."

Arthur paused for a second, picked up what appeared to be a framed photo and said, "Before you leave, I would like to read to you an anonymous poem which my daughter-in-law gave to my son as a gift:

> 'Many people speak of dreams
> as fanciful things
> like fairies' charmed rings and lands of enchantment.
>
> Others only believe in faraway dreams
> such as stars or sea castles
> with elf-like inhabitants.
>
> There are day-dreamers
> and night-dreamers
> who dream up make-believe places
>
> They use much imagination
> and in that are dream-gifted
> but the serious dreamers are those who catch dreams
> and bring them to life, to show
> that when they were dreaming, they meant it.'

My friends, you all have an opportunity to be dream makers. Keep this in mind as you read Melchior's story."

As Arthur exited the ballroom, Hartwell made one final announcement. "Ladies and gentlemen, please return your briefcases to me at 8:30 A.M. tomorrow. Thank you."

Scott settled comfortably into the lounge area of their suite. He sat in the embroidered wingback chair, set his cup of hot coffee on the antique desk with notepad and pen at hand. Even though he gave up smoking almost twenty years ago, he still enjoyed an occasional cigar on special occasions. This was one of those special occasions. He lit up the Monte

Cristo #2 which Arthur had presented to him before leaving the Boardroom.

He anxiously opened the briefcase. The letter which Arthur mentioned was on top of the brown package wrapped with twine. Scott read:

"Dear Scott,

It is with great pleasure that I welcome you to the fraternity of a select few who have been chosen over the centuries to carry on the legacy of Melchior. In his Memoirs you will read about his early travels visiting the Seven Wonders of the Ancient World. You will discover what he describes as the Greatest Wonder of All. You will learn the Precepts for Happiness which he espouses and finally you will come to understand why you have been invited to join us in this quest.

With very few exceptions for over two thousand years, those who have been invited, have accepted the challenge. Whether you do so or not, I ask only that you honor my following requests:

First, the manuscript which we have loaned to you is for your personal use. Do not show it to
anyone else other than Ellen.

Second, do not reproduce or copy any part of the manuscript.

Third, keep all these things which you have seen and heard this past weekend about Melchior in the strictest confidence.

Fourth, at the end of the memoirs, please sign your initials in agreement as the others before you have done.

Lastly, if you decide to join us, meet me in the boardroom at 9:00 A.M. tomorrow morning. If not , Karen and I wish you and your family all the best that life has to

offer. Perhaps our paths will cross again. Godspeed.
In friendship,
Arthur Kincaid III."

Scott hurriedly placed the letter back in the briefcase. He took out the package and placed it on the desk. Before proceeding any further, he stubbed out his Havana, concerned that he might accidentally drop hot ashes on this priceless document. He looked around self consciously feeling as if he had been caught sneaking cookies out of Gramma's forbidden cookie jar. Gingerly he undid the twine and removed the wrapping.

The book bound with copper studs was two inches thick. Hand engraved on the front of the brown leather cover, worn from constant use, were the words, "The Manuscripts of Melchior."

Immediately below the title there was a symbol burned deeply into the hide. It looked like a star shining down on a pine tree on a hill with the wind blowing. Scott, now completely focused on the task at hand, turned to the first page of the ancient parchment and began reading.

"The journal I leave has been recorded by my scribe, Petronius, who puts down my words in Greek and in Latin as I dictate to him.

I am Melchior, first born son of Nabodrezzar, descendant from the Royal Line of Hammurabi, King of Ancient Babylon...the lost empire in a world where Romans rule. I was born in the first year of the reign of Augustus, when Caesar was victorious over his arch rival Marc Antony and Cleopatra who dreamed of conquering the world…

I was born to be a king but I aspired to no such calling, believing deep in my soul that the trappings of kingship would enchain me no less than the four sided walls of the jailer's prison. My heart desired the freedom only knowledge can bring. I wanted to be one with the stars. I sought the adventure of travel. I longed to visit faraway lands, to see the wonders of the world. Against my father's wishes, I renounced my position as rightful heir to the throne and started on my journey."

Chapter Seven:

The First Wonder

Scott read on fascinated by the story unfolding.

"I traveled to Medina and thence onward to Mecca... across the Red Sea to my primary destination, the glory of Egypt... not for the wealth of the Nile that most travelers seek, but in search of the treasure of the Great Library of Alexandria. Here I found the wisdom of the ages bound up in scrolls.

I met a holy man, Hassan by name, once a priest of the Pharaoh, who now served as curator for the Library's collection of over five hundred thousand leather and papyrus scrolls. He introduced me to the writings of Homer, Plato, Herodotus, Cicero, Aristotle, Aristophanes, Virgil and Plautus. By day, I studied the great classics at my fingertips; at night, I studied the stars in the heavens and charted the course of planetary movements which might influence the course of history.

Hassan invited me to be a member of Alexandria's Museum, an institution established for academics to pursue their love of learning and where scholarship was rewarded by free food and lodging and even more surprisingly, an exemption from taxes. The Library and Museum were the intellectual points of light. Alexandria was famous for another point of light, a beacon for sailors and travelers, which was known as one of the Seven Wonders of the world: the Pharos, the Great Lighthouse of Alexandria."

Scott thought he had died and gone to heaven. Melchior's journal was turning out to be better than a crystal ball with a vision to the past. He kept on reading.

"Hassan told me the story of how Pharos, the island not far from the mouth of the Delta, got it's name. The beautiful Helen of Troy came to Egypt with her ill fated lover, Paris, and stayed in the small fishing village located on a narrow strip of land between the mountain and the sea.

One day while strolling through the village, Helen asked an old fisherman fixing his nets, 'What is the name of this island?'

He replied, 'It's the Pharoah's.'

This was in happier times, before Troy was destroyed by deception. The Trojans had accepted the gift of the Trojan Horse, a trick devised by Odysseus, King of Ithaca and comrade in arms to Menelaus, husband to Helen, the face that launched a thousand ships.

Hassan revealed that when Alexander the Great arrived in Egypt on his quest to conquer the Persian Satrap Darius, he marched from Memphis, the capital of Egypt, along the Nile to Rhacotis, the fishing village which Helen visited. Here he determined to build the greatest city of all, which would bear his name, Alexandria. On the island of Pharos, close to the entrance of the harbor of this great city, he would build a beacon such as the world had never seen, the first of its kind.

It would rise almost three hundred feet in the air and cast a light that could be seen for three hundred miles from every direction. At night the fires would burn without end, reflected by gigantic mirrors made from polished bronze. By day the sun's brightness sent out beacons of light as a symbol of welcome to the wayward sailor, the weary traveler or the homeward bound. This was the first wonder I saw, the

Pharos of Alexandria. This was the lesson in life I learned: that wisdom shines its light for every man.

Chapter Eight:

The Second Wonder

After studying the scrolls of Alexandria's library for almost a year, Hassan invited me and several other pilgrims living at the Museum to accompany him to see what Egypt was most famous for in the annals of history - the Great Pyramids. The triangular monuments dominate the skyline wherever one looks to the desert. The largest of these is numbered among the seven wonders of the world.

In preparation for our expedition, Hassan examined us on what we had learned about the construction of the pyramids from reading the descriptions put forth by the historians Herodotus, Diodorus and Strabo who specialized in geography.

"Let us begin with the easy questions first," Hassan announced, as he looked around at the pilgrims gathered about him.

"What are the 'Mountains of Pharoah'?"

Quick to answer was the student from Beijing, China, called Hup Jai. "They are the royal tombs of the Pharoahs."

"Where are they located?"

"Near the border of the Libyan desert on the plateau of Giza which is five miles from the Nile and thirteen and a half miles from Memphis." Kunta Bodunrin from Ethiopi responded, beaming from ear to ear with his pearly white teeth.

"Who built these monuments?"

"Khufu, Pharaoh of the fourth dynasty, or better known as Cheops. He built the first and the largest of the Pyramids at Giza. His successor, Khafra, built the second called 'Great is Chephren' and Menkaura followed with the third named 'Mykerinus is divine.'" Hassan nodded his approval at Hananias the disciple from Jerusalem who answered perfectly.

"When were these edifices built?"

"I know," offered Ahmed Sharif from Persia, "the Great Pyramid was completed around 2529 years before the reign of Augustus. The two smaller monuments were built approximately one hundred and three hundred and fifty years later."

"What was the size of the Great Pyramid?"

Jamil Baba from the city of Baghdad, who had just joined us, shouted, "511 feet high and…but…I can't remember the other dimensions."

Hassan's steely gaze bore right through Jamil Baba who lowered his head in shame.

Hananias broke the silence. "The sides are built at a slope of 54 degrees and extend 756 feet from top to bottom. The area covered by the 2,300,000 blocks is 13.1 acres. Each block weighed between 2 to 15 tons."

Again, Hassan looked at Hananias with approval. He continued his questions. "How long did it take to build?"

Noone spoke up.

"Hassan," Balthazar the Indian priest from Ceylon, interjected, "if you will allow me to answer?"

"By all means, Balthazar."

"Conservative estimates say that the number of people who worked on the Great Pyramid numbered about 360,000. The project took 20 years to complete. Herodotus tells us that the cost of just the radishes, onions and garlic consumed by the laborers was well over 1600 talents."

Scott paused, a furrow creasing his forehead. He quickly rummaged through his old leather satchel and pulled out his hand calculator. He figured out the value of the 1600 talents at present silver prices and came up with a figure of $12,500,000.00 dollars. Imagine what the cost of the total project would add up to, he thought.

Taking stock of what he had learned so far from the journal, Scott ran through the details in his mind. Some of the questions brought up in the symposium had already been answered. Melchior was indeed a king and came from Babylon. Balthazar, another of the Magi, was a priest who came from India. Melchior's memoirs was a gold mine of information. He picked up reading where he left off.

"Thank you, Balthazar. That brings us to the final two questions. How were the pyramids built and why?"

Gaspar, the Greek scholar with whom I had become fast friends over the past year, volunteered to explain how the Egyptians could build such a huge monument without the knowledge of the pulley which the Romans would invent 2500 years later.

"Several theories are proposed on how the Egyptians were able to build the tallest building in the world," Gaspar began. "One theory is that ramps were built that encircled the building. The higher the building rose, the higher the ramps were built, like scaffolding. Another theory suggests that a long ramp extending out into the desert was used. The higher the building rose, the longer and higher the ramp had to be made. The most popular theory is that the master builders used levers to raise each block to the nest level one step at a time and used rollers to move the blocks into place."

"Well spoken, Gaspar. And who will give us an answer to

the final question? Why were the pyramids built?"

Hassan looked directly at me.

Proudly I took up Hassan's challenge. "Egypt has a long standing tradition which required that a royal tomb be erected for each Pharaoh in succession. This royal tomb was constructed as the resting place for the body while the spirit soared to the great beyond. Kingship bestowed the responsibility on the Pharaoh to become a bridge for his people on earth to the gods in the other world who would send good fortune.

Some people question why there are more pyramids than pharaohs. The most common explanation is that two pyramids were often built for the pharaoh, "King of Upper and Lower Egypt, Lord of the Two Lands," which gave him a burial site in two areas. Others say that the second edifice was not built as a tomb but as a cenotaph, a hollow memorial without any provisions for a burial chamber.

I suggest that the building of pyramids was not just motivated by religious beliefs but also for political reasons. A wise King knows that the best way to motivate and inspire his people is through a common goal which unifies the nation. The creation of a monumental masterpiece which is admired throughout the world brings not only glory to the king, but pride and loyalty from his people."

Hassan nodded his approval and said we were ready for our journey.

The backdrop of the pyramids against the skyline of the morning sun when heaven and desert meet is indescribable. For centuries mankind has stood in awe of these monuments simply because of their immense size and solidarity. This was the second wonder I saw, the Great Pyramids of Egypt. This was the lesson in life I learned: the value of teamwork and a common goal - after which nothing is impossible.

Chapter Nine:

The Third Wonder

Heralds arrived in Egypt to announce the celebration of the Olympic games and to extend invitations to all the resident Greeks to participate in the contests. Gaspar, my Greek colleague, invited me to accompany him to Olympia to experience the pageantry and pomp of the competitions. I had always planned on going to Greece so I welcomed the opportunity to travel with Gaspar and some of the others to Athens and then join the thousands of travelers from all parts of the world who flocked to Olympia for the athletic contests. From Egypt and Syria, from Macedonia and Sicily, from Ephesos and all of Asia they would come. Tradition demanded that while the games were being held, all war would cease and for just a blessed moment in time, there was peace throughout the land.

"Gaspar," I asked, "how did the Olympic tradition begin?"

"As you might suspect, the athletic contests were originally just a part of a religious festival to honor the Greek god, Zeus. Some believe that Heracles, the son of Zeus and mighty hero to the people, established the games at Olympia in honor of his father. Others prefer to believe in the love story of Pelops who won Hippodameia's hand as the reason for the first Olympic games."

"Tell us, Gaspar," I said, "about the myth of Pelops."

"Gladly, Melchior. Let me begin by telling you of King

Oenomaus. To the west of the Pelopomese, in the southern part of Greece, lay Olympia, a land which was sacred to Zeus and where Mother Earth was rich and fertile. Farmers would come from afar to worship and seek divine help in making their own crops as abundant. This was part of the territory ruled by Oenomaus.

In time, a daughter, Hippodameia, was born to the King who cherished his new born child and watched her grow in strength and beauty. Unfortunately, Oenomaus in his pride and ignorance somehow offended the mighty Poseidon, god of the sea, who spat forth a riddle: 'Beware the upstart, who claims title to your heart.' Oenomaus believed that this was a prophecy which foretold his death by the hand of the one who would marry his beloved daughter.

As years passed, the time came when Oenomaus ran out of excuses. He could no longer put off the many suitors clamoring for the hand of Hippodameia. Then the king devised a plan. He issued a challenge to all would be suitors to prove their bravery and earn the right to the hand of his daughter. Every suitor had to agree to a chariot race from Olympia to the temple of Poseidon in Corinth, a race course of eighty miles. Each challenger would be given a head start and whoever was victorious would win Hippodameia and the throne. But, if he lost the race, he would also forfeit his life.

Despite the risk, thirteen suitors accepted the challenge. Thirteen suitors failed and paid with their lives, until one day, a handsome young man named Pelops appeared. Against all odds, he claimed his right to challenge Oenomaus in the race for a bride and a kingdom. No one knows for sure the reason for what happened next. Some say the god Poseidon took his vengeance on Oenomaus in full. Some say Pelops bribed the king's henchmen to sabotage his chariot. Others point to the expression of sadness on Oenamaus' face when he saw how happy Hippodameia was when she looked upon Pelops. Whatever the cause, Oenomaus died that day. His chariot overturned and his body was crushed. Pelops became king and wed Hippodameia.

Many Greeks believe that the introduction of chariot racing and other athletic contests were included in the festivities of Olympia to commemorate the courage of Pelops."

On our journey to his homeland, Gaspar entertained us with multiple tales of the Greek myths. He spoke about the gods and goddesses of Olympus, and the mighty heroes in war like Achilles, about the one-eyed monsters and three headed dragons, about witches and sirens, but it was the stories about love lost and won, like the one about Pelops and Hippodameia that captured our imagination and stirred our hearts."

Scott stopped reading and took a deep breath. He had to be dreaming. Was he actually reading these stories told by one of the three wisemen almost two thousand years ago? Again he reviewed the new information he gained. The third Magi, Gaspar, was a Greek from Athens. The three Magi obviously became friends at the Library of Alexandria and studied together. College buddies you might say. Can't stop now, he thought. got to keep reading.

"Balthazar, Kunta, HupJai and I reached the top of the knoll overlooking the temple at the same time. We waited for Gaspar and Jamil then raced down the slope and entered the temple. There we stared in amazement at the likeness of the god Zeus which was appropriately called the masterpiece of the sculptor Pheidias, renown for his artistry throughout the civilized world.

Pheidias portrayed Zeus sitting on his throne with is head

almost touching the ceiling of the temple which was at least 50 feet high. The statue itself was made entirely of ivory. In his left hand he held a staff, an eagle perched on top. In his right hand sat a figurine of the winged Goddess also made of ivory.

Placed on top of his head, was the symbol of victory in the Olympic Games, the wreath of olive sprays. The robe of Zeus and his sandals appeared to be made of ivory and gold. Precious stones of every color were inlaid throughout the massive art work including the throne itself.

Pheidias had created a likeness of the god which included all of the aspects assigned to him, especially the description which Homer gave when he described Zeus as the austere one who by just a nod of his head would cause the whole of Mount Olympus to tremble. This was the third wonder I saw, the Statue of Zeus at Olympia. This was the lesson in life I learned, the value of competition and especially persistence - the most important ingredient for success.

Chapter Ten:

The Fourth Wonder

All of us who had met at the Library of Alexandria, who studied together and lived together, shared a common goal. We were determined to seek not just the knowledge recorded on leather and papyrus but to learn the wisdom of the ages by visiting the far corners of the world, by experiencing all that different lands and different peoples had to offer, and most importantly, to sit at the feet of the most learned men of all time to absorb their teachings. We shared a vision that one day we might gather all of the information together like the Great Library and share this with all who wished to be enlightened.

To this end, we made a pact. No matter how far apart we traveled, we would serve notice to one another and gather for a symposium so that we could share the lessons we had learned. Messages would be sent by courier pigeons that roam the skies for hundreds of miles in a single day. They would keep us abreast of important news. Our first symposium would be in my homeland of Babylon, a year from this day.

And so we parted as friends and colleagues, with a common mission.

Balthazar, Hananias, Jamil and Omar set sail from the Sea of Rome west toward the Ocean of Darkness to the Rock of Gibraltar. Gaspar, Kunta, HupJai and I traveled north to the Black Sea and down to Ephesus on a journey which would eventually lead me back to where I first started, my homeland of Babylon.

Scott paused. Excitedly he related all that he had read to Ellen. She had not seen such enthusiasm in her husband for such a long time. Silently she gave thanks that Scott had been included in the symposium. He resumed reading the manuscript.

Kunta explained that one of the tasks assigned to him by the elders of his homeland in Ethiopia was to inspect the most beautiful architecture in the world.

Gaspar exclaimed, "Then we must visit the Temple of Artemis which has been called Graecae Magnificae."

HupJai added, "Next in line, I recommend that we go to see the Mausoleum at Halicarnassus."
And so our journey's path was determined. First to Ephesus, then down the coast of Turkey to Halicarnassus. We planned on taking a boat to the island of Rhodes to see for ourselves the 'Colossus' which many say is so high it touches the heavens.

Hananias had encouraged us to spend time at Damascus and his birthplace, the city of Jerusalem or as some call it the center of the world. He gave us the name of his uncle whom he believed to be old in age and also in wisdom.

Hupjai insisted that we all continue our journey from Jerusalem to Baghdad then to Mecca, follow the inlet of the Indian Ocean to Sri Lanka and voyage by ship on the Unchartered Ocean to Bejing, land of his forefathers.

Along the way we shared stories of our childhood.

Gaspar instructed us about the myth of the virgin goddess Artemis, daughter of Zeus and twin sister to the sun god, Apollo.

"The Greeks believed that Artemis roamed the mountains and the forests, serving as protector to the weak and

defenseless. Legend tells us how she punished the great King
Agamemnon, leader of all the Greek forces in the war against
Troy, because he killed a deer, which was one of her favorite
animals. For his crime, Agamemnon found his fleet stranded
in the harbor without wind for his sails until he appeased the
goddess.

Perhaps this is why the Temple also gained fame throughout
the land as a refuge for suppliants who came from far and
wide to seek sanctuary. The goddess granted asylum to all
who came within her domain. No one dared ignore the law
of sanctuary. Even foreign enemies took advantage of the law.
The Persian King Xerxes, after he was defeated by the Greeks,
sent his children to the temple for safety.

The most fascinating story is told about the legendary
Amazons, the tribe of female warriors who were descended
from Ares, the god of war. During the Trojan war, they had
fought against the Greeks. Fearful of retaliation by the victors,
they sought asylum at the temple. The Amazons were so well
received, that a contest was held in their honor. Sculptors
were invited to create bronze statues of the Amazons. Four of
the best art works were kept in the temple as a symbolic truce
between east and west."

Scott's excitement grew as he read further on about
Melchior's journey to Ephesus. He remembered visiting the
site of the temple as a young archeology graduate student. It
was his first field experience. His thoughts drifted back to the
words of Professor William Swanson who had brought his
students to this place.

"Here is where practical archeology began. It was 1860
when John Wood spent seven years digging in the mud of
this wet plain and found the foundation of this temple.
Until then, for the love of god, I don't know why, all of

our knowledge was based solely on the written records left by the Greeks and Romans: History, Mythology, Science, Mathematics. Why no historian or scholar ever thought to dig in the ground to unearth these architectural treasures until Wood is unbelievable. But once it started, it was a continuous race of discovery. Only ten years after Wood, Schliemann discovered the legendary walls of Troy."

Scott knew that he would now find out more about the temple in one page than all the archaeological expeditions had found in a hundred years.

"The temple was a large rectanglar structure surrounded on all sides by hundreds of stark white pillars. The light of the sun reflected by the marble building blinded us so that we had to shield our eyes with our cloaks. We climbed up the marble steps surrounding the entire structure and entered a large courtyard open to the heavens. The court which contained the altar was encased by forests of columns decorated with elaborate friezes.

The tapered columns were at least sixty feet high. The platform itself looked to be about 250 feet wide and twice as long. In front of the center door on either side were two bronze statues of the Amazons. As we entered the sacred chamber down the rows of central columns, we saw the interior house of the goddess situated in the center of the building fronted and backed by two rows of statues. The figure of Artemis herself dominated the mind's eye. Here was the finest example of the Greek's view of the temple as the house of the soul.

This was the fourth wonder I saw, the Temple of Artemis at Ephesis. This was the lesson in life I learned: mankind has an indomitable thirst for the divine and for the meaning of existence.

Chapter Eleven:

The Fifth Wonder

Scott shook his head in disbelief recalling the story of the blind men who tried to define an elephant only by the individual parts they could feel: one passed his hand over the elephant's leg and described this creature as a thick coconut tree that moves up and down; another felt the tail of the beast and called it a rope; the third blind man, feeling the elephant's trunk believed it to be a huge snake which could crush it's prey. Were the scholars who studied the ancient remains and records also blind in their approach, Scott mused? So much attention was paid to the little details without stepping back and seeing the whole picture. A lesson to be learned perhaps. He picked up the journal and continued reading.

Kunta was ecstatic over the architectural wonders of the Temple of Artemis and talked incessantly about sharing his discovery with his elders when he returned home. He could not wait until we arrived at Halicarnassus to view the Mausoleum.

In the meantime, HupJai volunteered to entertain us with a story from his homeland. He talked about the legendary "Eight Immortals" who were heroes in Chinese folklore. They served as role models for ordinary people to follow since they had found enlightenment. Their reward was the gift of immortality. They did not become gods as it were but had super human powers, used magic and flew through the air with lightning speed. Their mission was to conquer evil throughout the world.

Sitting around the campfire, looking up at the stars, we talked of many things and opened our souls to one another.

The journey to Halicarnassus from Ephesus was not long. Gaspar once more provided the background information for us before we arrived at the Mausoleum.

"Maussollos, son of Hekatomnos, Governor for the King of Persia, moved the capital of his kingdom from Mylasa to the coastal town of Halicarnassus for his wife Artemisia. Its seems his new bride loved the seashore, the sight of the sails in the harbor and the golden hues of the sky as the sun set over the ocean. For Artemesia, he would do anything.

In return for his devotion, Artemisia vowed to build a memorial in his name so large and so elaborate that it would rival the great pyramids of Egypt. To this end, she recruited the most famous sculptors and assigned them a specific task: Bryaxis would design and create sculptures for the north wall, Timotheus was given the south side, those on the east would be carved by Scopas, and for the west, Leochares was chosen. Above all, Pythis was given the responsibility of creating the artwork which would adorn the summit of the Mausoleum.

Before the structure was built, Queen Artemisia joined her husband in death. But as a testament of their loyalty to the queen and to their own artistic endeavor, the artisans did not stop the work until the monument was completed."

Scott smiled to himself as he thought of Artemisia's vow. The monument she built in memory of her husband no longer stood in splendor like the pyramids of Egypt, but her creation had been so magnificent that his name lives on as a generic term for any large tomb today - the Mausoleum.

Melchior's journal continued, "As everyone expected, Kunta ran ahead to be the first to view what many believed to be the master artwork of the ages. HupJai with his short bowed legs was out of breath when he joined us, staring open mouthed at the edifice before us.

Multiple steps led up to the large podium base which was decorated with life size figures of Greek and Persian warriors engaged in battle, some of whom were on horseback. On the second level, stationary statues of male and female heroes were lined up in a row in counterpoint to the action scenes of the podium below and the series of action scenes of animal hunts, Centaurs, Amazons and the heroic exploits of Theseus on the third level. The fourth story featured free standing portraits of Maussollos, Artemisia and their ancestors. Interspersed between these statues was a series of tall ionic columns which supported the fifth level decorated with twelve colossal lion statues. On this story, a pyramid shaped tower was built an additional forty feet high crowned with Pythis' masterpiece, a four horse drawn chariot.

This was only one side of the rectangular structure which soared about one hundred and fifty feet above the ground. We slowly walked around the four sides of the tomb and admired the beauty and skill of its creators. Surely, it deserved its place among the other ancient masterpieces.

This was the fifth wonder I saw, the Mausoleum at Halicarnassus. This was the lesson in life I learned: the value of loyalty, devotion and friendship.

Chapter Twelve:

The Sixth Wonder

W e decided to leave our horses and backpacks with an innkeeper in the town of Halicarnassus. Down at the docks, Kunta found a young boat captain whom we persuaded to sail us to the island of Rhodes. The island was situated right in the middle of the sea-lane between Greece and Cyprus which was a boon to its commercial success.

Kunta was anxious to show off the information he had gained from discourse with some of the people he had met on our journey.

"So tell us, Kunta," I said, "what is so special about Rhodes?"

Grinning from ear to ear, Kunta launched into the history of the island which impressed even Gaspar, the scholar.

"After the death of Alexander the Great in the 292nd year before the reign of Augustus Caesar, his generals divided the empire between themselves: Ptolemy I of Egypt and Antigonous, King of Macedonia. Antigonous entreated the leaders of Rhodes to join him in his conquest over Egypt. They refused. In retaliation, Antigonous commanded his son Demetrius, the Sacker of Cities, to launch an attack against the island. This is the legendary story of how a small village fought for freedom and defeated the mighty despot - a David and Goliath battle.

Demetrius assembled a mighty armada of 300 warships and half as many transport ships to land over 50,000 warriors with a support staff of twice a many men. He brought with him weapons of destruction made specifically to overcome the staunchest defenders and to lay low the strongest walls: armored towers, catapults, battering rams, slingers and the most sophisticated engines of war ever created. Yet, after one full year, the siege failed to discourage the defenders of freedom from their mission. The islanders looked death in the face and did not back down.

Demetrius was so impressed by their courage, he called off the attack and offered to negotiate a truce. A treaty was agreed to by both sides. Henceforth, the Rhodians would be an ally of Demetrius against all except Egypt, but most importantly, the island of Rhodes would keep its independence.

"Bravo, Kunta," said Gaspar, "but what can you tell us of the Colossus?"

"Demetrius in a token gesture of friendship left all of his weapons of war for the Rhodians. They in turn sold it for a large sum. With this money, they decided to create the largest statue ever made, a masterpiece fashioned in the likeness of their protector, Helios, the sun god. Chares, the sculptor chosen unanimously, took twelve years to cast the bronze figure seven times ten cubits high plus ten, which stood at the entrance to the five harbors of Rhodes as a symbol to all about the fight for a fee and independent people."

Kunta took out a small fragment and waved it in the air. He explained it was a copy of a poem which was carved into the base of the statue:

"To you, oh Sun, the people of Dorian Rhodes set up this bronze statue reaching to Olympus, when they had pacified the waves of war and crowned their city with the spoils taken from the enemy. Not only over the seas but also on land did they kindle the lovely torch of freedom and independence.

For to the descendants of Heracles belongs dominion over sea and land.”

We arrived at the harbor where we disembarked. HupJai chattered incessantly about not seeing the Colossus from the sea.

“After we disembarked from our ship, Gaspar led us to the center of the five harbors and there on a promontory was a mound on top of which there was something that looked to be a giant pedestal. As we walked around the mound, we were all startled to see the massive Colossus face down in the ground, broken at the knees. I could see the tears well up in HupJai’s eyes as we all approached the fallen titan. Where the limbs were torn asunder, huge chasms revealed the tremendous amount of rock which the sculptor used to fill the cavity. Gaspar stood in the opening, stretched out his arms above his head to its full height and could not touch the top of the giant’s belly. Even sprawled on the ground, it was a marvel to behold. Kunta could not encircle his arms around the thumb of the giant. The fingers alone were larger that most life size statues.

HupJai finally found himself asking us to explain, “What happened? Who destroyed the Colossus? Why?”

Gaspar explained, “Some say the god Poseidon caused the ocean to topple the image of Helios. Others claim it was an earthquake from the bowels of Mother Earth which brought the mighty Titan to his knees. Because of the island’s loyalty over the years, Ptolemy, the Pharaoh of Egypt, offered to rebuild the statue. But the islanders declined his offer.

This was the sixth wonder I saw, the Colossus of Rhodes. This was the lesson in life that I learned: the value of freedom - a testament to the human spirit to overcome all adversity.

Chapter Thirteen:

The Seventh Wonder

We picked up our caravan where we had left it at Halicarnassus and traveled to Damascus first, then down the coast to Jerusalem, the city that Solomon built. Here we aspired to learn more of the Jewish traditions and to study their sacred texts. We were eager to listen to the priests and scholars as they gathered in the temple and read from their holy books.

Remembering Hanania's's recommendation, we sought out his uncle, Joram, who was a member of the Sanhedrin. Joram was a wonderful host. He made every effort to accommodate our desires and made sure we had access to the temple and to the library where we were able to study the ancient scriptures.

One night during the evening meal, Kunta asked Joram to tell us the story of the legendary Solomon, son of King David.

"Everyone knows of David's exploits against the giant Goliath," said Kunta, "but will you share with us how it came to pass, that Solomon has always been called the wisest of men?"

Joram began, "Solomon was very young when he became King, but already he showed great promise and maturity. To keep the peace, he married the daughter of his chief enemy, the Pharaoh of Egypt and had his rival Adonijah executed. Still, young Solomon was troubled. One night, after a great religious celebration, the Lord God asked Solomon in a dream. "What gift do you desire above all else?" Solomon thought long and hard before he gave his answer. "Lord, I wish to be a good and just ruler. I wish to treat my people with fairness in all things and to be able to distinguish between good and evil. Grant me the gift of wisdom, Lord, so that I may serve you and my people well the rest of my days."

And the Lord was pleased. "Solomon," he said, "you have answered well. Because you did not ask for something just for yourself but for something that would benefit your people, I will grant you your wish. I will also give you the rewards of wealth, long life and the honor deserving of a wise man." And so it came to pass that Solomon became famous not just for building the temple of Jerusalem but for his wisdom, evidenced by the hundreds of poems and song s collected in the Book of Proverbs."

And so we passed our time in Jerusalem studying the scrolls by day. At night we sat at the table of Joram and listened to his stories about the history of his people. He told us of Solomon's fall and how the kingdom was split into two: Israel in the north and Judah to the south. He talked about the exile of the Israelites and the destruction of the city after being conquered by my ancestors, the Babylonians led by King Nabuchadnezzar. We were fascinated by the stories of Daniel and the Lions, of the beautiful Esther, in stark contrast to the evil Jezebel. We listened attentively to the description of Jonah and the Whale and the Dream of Nebuchadnezzar. But it was the stories about the ancient prophets that captivated us the most. He introduced us to Elijah and the Chariot of Fire. He told us about Jeremiah and Ezekiel but it was clear that Isaiah to whom he referred as 'the eagle among all the prophets,' was his favorite.

Joram became excited when he quoted from Isaiah who had foretold the birth of the Messiah, descended from the House of David and destined to be the Savior of all the Jewish people.

"Isaiah tells us in the holy book: 'For unto us a child is born, unto us a son is given: and the law shall be upon His shoulder: and His name shall be called Counselor, the mighty God, the everlasting Father, the Prince of Peace.'"

We found many other sayings of the prophets in the ancient scriptures talking about their Messiah and we were intrigued by the mystery of their total confidence that this would come to pass.

Many new moons had come and gone and it was time to venture forth once again on our travels. It was difficult to say goodbye to the scholars and priests who had befriended us during our stay in Jerusalem. Only the excitement of new adventures and opportunities which lay ahead stirred us out of our comfortable sojourn. So we bade Farewell to Joram and his colleagues, promising that we would surely meet again in the not too distant future.

From the center of the world, we could choose any number of roads. To the west lay the Ocean of Darkness and Morocco where our friends led by Balthazar had ventured, to the east was the Uncharted Ocean where sits the crowded cities of China at the edge of the world. We chose the road to Baghdad with plans to continue on to the Persian Gulf where we would board ship to India and beyond.

On our journey through a mountain pass we were attacked by robbers. Kunta and I who were trained in battle drew our swords to fight off the thieves. HupJai did his share of damage using a strange form of fighting with his feet. Our attackers, not expecting such a defense, retreated in disarray.

Just as I turned with my arms raised in victory, their leader shot a arrow which pierced my left side damaging the lung and breaking some of the rib bones. Gaspar, our emergency physician, proved his mettle in treating my wound and the others who were injured. Some of our attendants were killed in the melee, and we lost several of our backpack mules.

Of necessity, our plans were altered so that we decided to head directly to Babylon where I could receive medical treatment and recuperation. The journey east to the land of heaven-colored silk and rice paddies would have to be without me.

Our caravan slowly made its way following the Tigris River as it flows south down to the junction where it meets the rush of the Euphrates. Here Gaspar insisted that we set up camp to tend to my wound because I had lost a lot of blood. A messenger had been sent ahead to my father to advise him of our predicament.

A day after we set up camp, Joachim our family physician arrived with a retinue of guards to escort us home. He examined my wound and extracted small slivers of wood and metal which had broken off from the arrow that pierced my body and left my spirit weak.

It was dusk when we reached the grassy knoll overlooking my home. It had been seven years since I said farewell to my family and friends to seek adventure and enlightenment. We entered the city through the old Ishtar gate, moving steadfastly along the Processional Way. Just then, Kunta yelled out, "Look there! See the lights."

Gaspar and HupJai helped lift my head from the makeshift cot the doctor had made for me. I saw in the distance on the cliff where our palace was built hundreds of candles burning brightly as a welcome for my return. My thoughts raced ahead to the faces of my father and mother and my younger brother. Surely I had traveled the world but had never found any lights that were brighter than the lights of home.

Held in the bosom of my mother I learned that my father and my younger brother had died three years earlier, killed by rebels from the region south of Ur. I wept for myself and for those who never had a chance to see the faces of their loved ones again before they passed from this life on earth to their final destination.

For the next several weeks I gained my strength through the caring nurses who tended to my needs, especially the one called Esther. Gaspar had sent word to our friends traveling in the west about my injury so it was not unexpected when they all showed up at our door one day: Balthazar, Hananias, Jamil and Omar.

We determined to make the most of our reunion together and so we studied the charts of the skies for which our elders were famous and listened to the tales of the wise men of my hometown. They talked of the legendary gardens which our ancestor Nebuchadnezzar had built for his wife Amytis. The Median princess who was forced to wed the king as part of a political alliance made it clear that he could
ravish her body but he would never win her heart. The more she resisted the King's advances, the more enamored he became of her and so he vowed he would do anything to gain her love. He gave her the most exquisite gifts of jewels and gold. He built her a magnificent palace with furnishing from around the world. He commissioned artists to create the most beautiful statues and pictures for her delight. He had seamstresses fashion her clothing from honey colored silk from China, furs from Africa, linen from Egypt. Still, she demured.

Finally, as he knew she was homesick for the green valleys and mountain tops of her homeland, he determined to recreate nature's wonder for her. At first sight of the beautiful hanging gardens, Amytis wept in the King's arms, opening her heart to her husband who had kept his promise.

As soon as I was fit enough, I promised to take our friends on a tour to see for themselves the legendary gardens built for Queen Amytis many years ago.

Not far from the outskirts of the city where a tributary of the Tigris flows through the rocky mountains, there is a passageway large enough for a rider on horse or donkey to pass through in single file. After passing a stretch of uninhabited wasteland, I led my comrades through this hidden tunnel into a canyon not accessible by any other means. Sheer cliffs on either side of the chasm provided a fortress like protection from any outsiders attempting to scale the mountain.

Against the stark gray backdrop of the cliffs, the lush green beauty of the gardens struck any weary traveler with awe - like an oasis in the desert. This was truly an island paradise. As a young boy my father had shown me the way to the gardens, kept secret for so long - Amytis' private hideaway. At the time, I was more enthralled with the mystery of it all. Now seeing the gardens through the eyes of my friends, I realized I was really seeing it for the first time.

From a distance, one would assume that it was a grove of forest trees which sprung up out of the sheer sides of the cliffs. The trees looked to be more than twelve feet in circumference and fifty feet tall. As we approached closer we noticed the thick man made walls constructed of brick and asphalt - covered with earth so deep it could hold the roots of the largest trees. Stairways wound from the ground level to the upper terraces throughout the celebrated garden. Water brought forth from a canal flowed down from the top into ponds which then cascaded like waterfalls from each level to the level below bathing the pomegranate trees heavy with fruits and with life giving nourishment.

Trees and plants of every kind and color draped each ascending gallery which rose little by little so that it resembled the rise of a theatre. Here the stars in the drama were the colorful flowers and the tall grass kept green because of the constant irrigation of the water trickling through the entire complex supported by walls twenty feet thick. No greater artwork could be imagined than this combination of nature and man's ingenuity. A gift of love from a husband to his wife.

This was the seventh wonder I saw, the Hanging Gardens of Babylon. This was the lesson in life I learned the value of a special place which renews the body and comforts the soul - a place we can call home."

Chapter Fourteen:

A Symposium On Love

Scott felt his pulse racing. This was unbelievable This journal of Melchior was the answer to all of his dreams. The crowning point of his career. He held in his hand the answer to so many questions which had been asked over the centuries. Finally, he could put all of the doubt to rest. The cynics had always questioned the very existence of the Hanging Gardens of Babylon. And what of the other ancient Wonders of the World? Scott now knew more that a hundred and fifty years of archaeological digs had uncovered. He could publish the find of the century. Smiling smugly he focused on the next page.

We spent many nights searching the skies for new stars, new constellations and charted the rise and fall of the planets. We shared the knowledge of our Babylonian ancestors with the extensive records from China which HupJai brought with him. The others who studied the heavens were Balthazar, Omar, Hananias and Jamil. Kunta, exasperated by his inability to make out the clusters of stars which we named after the Greek heroes, chose to study his architectural drawings instead.

Gaspar, on the other hand, proudly announced he was more interested in the celestial bodies on earth rather that in the heavens and suggested we celebrate with a symposium dealing with the topic of Love.

Everyone joined in agreement and decided that it would

be a fitting farewell party before continuing the journey to the land of plump orchards at the eastern edge of the world.

The celebration continued late into the night. We had feasted to our hearts content on the finest delicacies grown and raised in the land of Babylon and consumed the nectar squeezed from the vines of the Hanging Gardens.

As host for the evening, I welcomed everyone to our debate and offered a toast for good fortune to all of our friends on their upcoming journey. In the tradition of the learned Plato, each guest was given a turn to talk at length on the topic of choice. My responsibility was to select the favorite argument put forth.

HupJai volunteered to be the first to speak. He espoused the lifestyle of China's emperors who typically had one hundred wives and an untold number of concubines. Tradition encouraged that a man take to himself as many wives as he could afford. This would give him many sons and daughters and create a strong family.

Kunta confirmed that this was also true in the villages of his people. Jamil and Omar also shared the same opinion.

Balthazar, the eldest of the group, spoke up, "I suggest that there is another perspective to this emotion - a different plane which is good and beautiful. For example, the love of a mother for her child or the love of a friend for a friend and most especially the love of a husband for his wife in old age. This manifests the spiritual part of man and is part of his heritage."

"Thank you, Balthazar," I said, "I am sure I speak for everyone here when I tell you that what you say is true. I suspect that this wisdom comes more easily with the enhancement of years."

Looking around the room to see who would speak next,

I noticed everyone pointing to Hananias. "What say you, Hananias? What opinion do you hold on the secret of love?"

Before he could speak, Omar interjected, "I dare say, Hananias will have more success convincing us that there is only one god than that man was created to enjoy only one woman!"

After the good natured laughter died down, Hananias, a deep furrow on his forehead, began to speak very softly so that the group became very quiet. "Honestly, I do not know the answer. Neither did our legendary Solomon, who despite his wisdom in all things else, surely failed in his search for happiness with women. For not one of his hundreds of wives brought him fulfillment but instead they were the cause which brought forth the wrath of the Lord and the splitting of his kingdom into two.

Yes, my friends, I readily confess I have no answer. Why is it so that a man who is surrounded by dozens of female companions can still feel so alone? Can a man find happiness in the arms of a woman who shares his bed but not his dream? Where is this elusive love, that Balthazar cherishes, to be found? I have not the answer."

My outspoken friend Gaspar was the last to speak.

"Ah, but I shall prove to you why this love you inquire about is so elusive, Hananias. I have our friend the playwright Aristophanes to thank for his wonderful explanation on the origin of true love. I beg his indulgence for adapting his myth to our purposes.

Let me begin my story. Long ago in the dawn of time before the age of heroes and titans, the nature of the human race was not the same as it is today. No, they were twice the size and twice as powerful. Imagine, if you will, the shape of each person as a rounded whole with back, front and sides forming a complete circle. Each human had four arms, four legs and two identical faces on a circular neck. There was only one head for both of these faces which were turned in opposite directions. Of course, you can imagine, based on everything I have said so far, that they had four ears, four eyes, two noses and two sets of genitals. They moved about in any direction as they wanted, walking upright on four limbs. But when they wanted to move faster, they did cartwheels on all eight limbs going round and round like the acrobatic tumblers.

Each generation became more powerful than the preceding one, more terrible than their parents before them and they multiplied and filled the earth - becoming more hateful with great ambition. Finally, in their pride, they thought themselves greater than the mighty gods of Olympus, and presumed to attack heaven itself.

Zeus, king of the gods, was so angry his first reaction was to strike all of humankind with devastating thunderbolts and destroy them as he did the giants before them. Hera, goddess of the hearth and queen of all the gods, advised compassion, reminding her strong willed husband that if the gods wiped out the human race then who would worship them and pay homage with their sacrifices which were pleasing to all of the gods. Many of the Olympian deities agreed with Hera.

"But what shall we do then with these arrogant creatures who have lost all semblance of gratitude?" complained Zeus.

'I have an idea, my father,' suggested Athena, goddess of wisdom. 'My plan will allow the humans to exist but they will be too weak to continue their obnoxious behavior. Cut each of them into two. They will become weaker and since they can only walk around upright on two legs, they will be less able to provoke war. There will also be twice as many of them - all the more to pay us tribute. If we find that they are still too aggressive we can cut them in two again so that they have to hop around on one leg.'

Zeus nodded his head approvingly while all the other gods joined in celebration of his decision. 'So let it be done.'

Immediately, the god Apollo was sent down to earth to halve each human into two like the cook cuts hardboiled eggs with a single string of hair. As each human was divided in two, Apollo, at Zeus' instructions, turned each face and neck attached to it around to the side with the gash so that each human would see their wound and remember their crime and punishment. In order that they would heal more quickly, Apollo gathered all the loose skin and stretched it tight in the middle of the belly - like the money changer who pulls his coin purse tight with a drawstring - and sewed it all together in the spot we now call the bellybutton. One last thing Apollo decided to do was smooth out all the wrinkles like the shoemaker who works on old leather in his workshop. And the gods saw what was done and they were content.

Of course, as the gods should have realized, since the original nature of humankind was now split in two, each half longed to be reunited with its other half. They wound their arms around each other tight trying to recombine into one single living being. No half would leave the other and if one were separated from the other, they would languish in depression, they would not eat and so they died from hunger. Concerned that the race would soon become extinct, Zeus took pity on them and at Athena's suggestion, he moved their genitals around to the front - instead of their backs where they were in the beginning - so that they could now reproduce themselves - the male and female together whenever they were intertwined together in unison. This would ensure the continuation of the human race.

"So you see, Hananias," Gaspar concluded, "every human being is always looking for it's other half. Only when a man finds his one true partner, or soulmate, can he be satisfied that he is complete. This is the secret of that elusive love which Balthazar suggests is true happiness."

Gaspar bowed several times to the raucous applause - the wine no doubt unleashing a freedom of spirit to the festivities - and so I said, "Once again there is no need to discuss whose story wins the popular vote and so we give Gaspar his due and our appreciation for the entertainment. But it is to Balthazar that we owe a tribute of thanks for sharing with us an important key to man's search for meaning in life - and to Hananias for posing the questions we sometimes are reluctant to ask." Everyone agreed in unison.

"We have come full circle, my friends, you and I together. Tomorrow we will take different paths, you to continue the quest which we started on our travels throughout the lands, and I to discover the secrets of happiness in the land where I was given life. May the gods protect you and bring you back safely until we meet again."

Scott came to the end of the page and let it all sink in - were the secrets of happiness as elusive to the wisest of men in days of old as they are to us today? Did mankind ever have that special knowledge? Can we ever find it or are we destined to search in vain for that pot of gold at the end of the rainbow? He anxiously turned the page and started the next chapter.

Chapter Fifteen:

Life's Blessing

The years have passed by quickly - happy years since I have found my mission in life. I fill my days doing something that I like to do, leading my people by example and teaching them the truth which I have discovered. At night I search the stars in all their wonder knowing that they have a message for us which is our task to unravel. I look forward to our symposium which have become well known far and wide. In addition to our original group of eight, many travelers come from as far away as a thousand miles seeking to hear the discourse of the Magi as we have come to be called.

I have chosen Solomon as my guide for his great wisdom in politics, in law, in architecture and in knowledge of all things except for that of womankind. In that I have followed my heart and have found my other half as Gaspar likes to call her. I made the choice to take as my one and only wife the beautiful Esther who once nursed me back to health after my injury suffered at the hands of bandits. She is the one who gave me back my strength, the one who gave me my beloved children, the one I call my blessing in life.

I am the descendant of kings. I was born a king, but there is no joy in kingship as I realized even as a young man. Every man must find his true calling from within. By the grace of God, he is truly blest if he finds someone to share it with always.

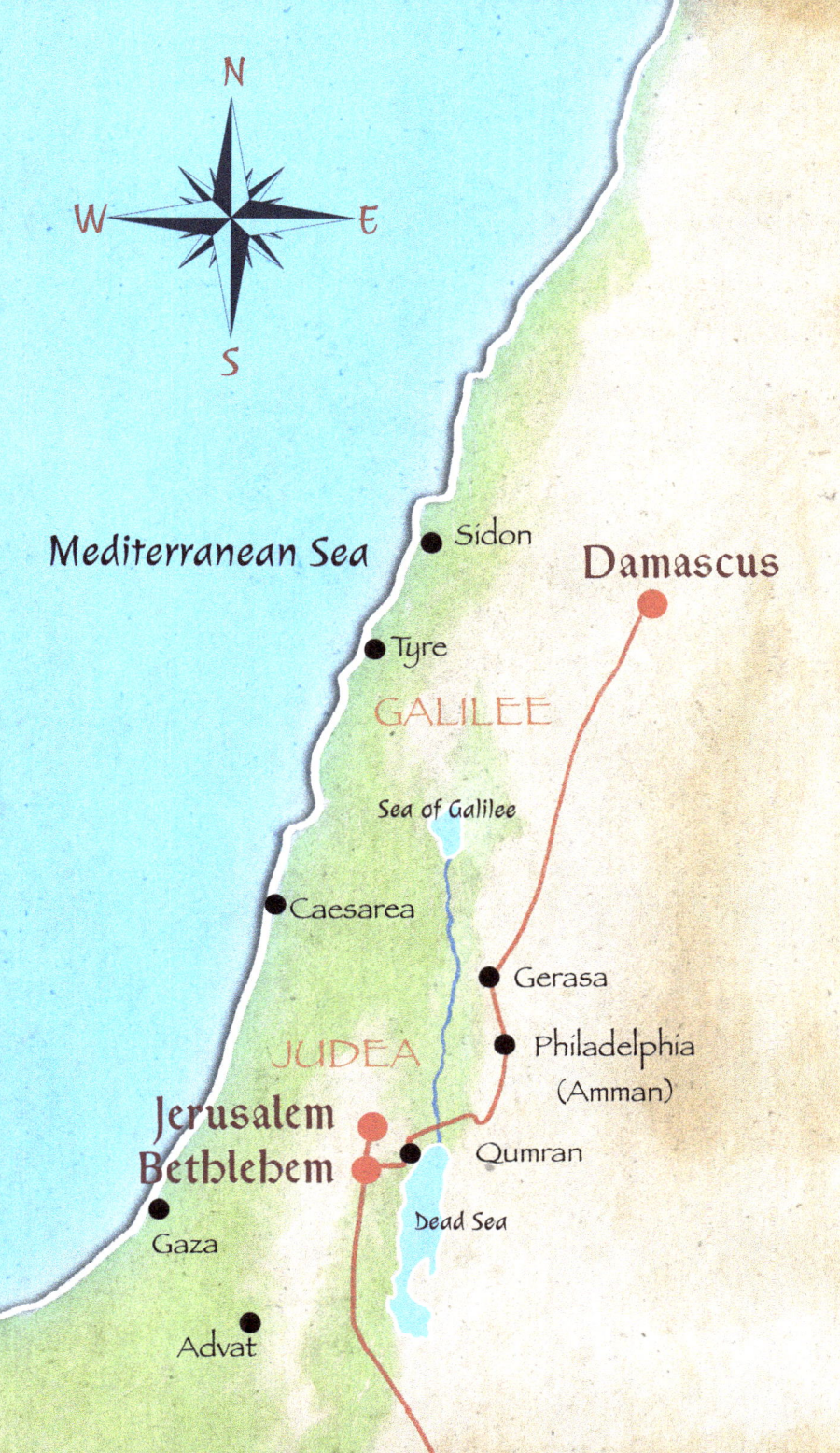

Chapter Sixteen:

The Greatest Wonder

On the tenth day after the Ides of March in the twenty sixth year of the reign of Augustus, I saw a coming together of the three planets Jupiter, Saturn and Mars. Our historical records tell of just such an occurrence and predict that it only happens every eight hundred years of so. I remembered HupJai mentioning such a conjunction recorded in the Chinese astronomical charts.

Excitedly I sent messages to our colleagues. They all responded that they too had seen this unusual occurrence and wondered whether this was the harbinger of something momentous. The month passed. We searched the skies expectantly but in vain. Word came to me that Hananias, Omar and Jamil were embarking on a ship down the Mediterranean to the Indian Ocean, making their way to the Ocean of Ignorance up to Beijing to study the detailed manuscripts of China's greatest scholars with HupJai in his homeland. Gaspar and Balthazar were on their way to join me in Babylon. Kunta was engaged in directing the building of a temple at the base of the Rubenzori Mountains and would join us as soon as he was able.

Eight months to the day of the first occurrence, Balthazar who had the first sky watch woke us hurriedly to see for ourselves the amazing display of heaven's delight. The darkness had turned into the light of day and our eyes were finally opened to the meaning of the dying star's intense blaze of glory - the dawn of a new age was about to begin.

In the twilight of darkness during the time when dreams crowd out deep sleep, I tossed and turned burning with a hot fever, not of the body, but of utter frustration in my mind as to the meaning of the celestial message we had seen.

"My husband," Esther whispered, "what is troubling thee? You know that you must follow the star wherever it may lead you. We will always be here waiting for you in Babylon, the city of your birth."

My spirit soared at the last words which my wife spoke. I now knew the secret which the heavens proclaimed so boldly. The time of prophecy was at hand. The star pointed to the kingdom of my wife's ancestors and the coming of the Messiah - the Savior, the newborn King of the Jews. Yes, it was no coincidence that Tiberius Caesar had issued a decree that all people would report to the city of their birth to be enrolled in the census. Thousands of pilgrims were traveling now back to the original city of their forefathers. The prophecy would be fulfilled.

Quickly I gathered Gaspar and Balthazar and many of our people and told them of my plan. We must journey to Jerusalem to find Hananias's uncle and tell him of our search. We must follow the bright star west to the land of Solomon and David to bear witness to the coming of this royal babe whose birth was foretold by the prophets of old.

Our caravan of horses, mules and camels loaded down with supplies proceeded steadily through the desert and countryside. We avoided the mountain passes where experience had taught us bandits and robbers lay in hiding for traveling merchants. Even Balthazar who usually complained about not having enough rest stops urged his camel onward with determination We rested during the heat of the day when the sun was at its highest and traveled during the night following the brightness of the star in the heavens which pointed the way to Jerusalem.

On the twelfth day from the beginning of our journey we arrived at the city of Baghdad - the halfway point to our final destination. We spoke with many pilgrims who were coming and going to the land of Judah because of Caesar's decree but did not find anyone with whom we believed we could share the excitement of our mission.

With our animals rested and fed, our supplies replenished and our enthusiasm overflowing, we set out following the heavenly guide ahead of us. On the twenty fourth day of our expedition, our beacon deserted us. We were fearful that the intensity of our star which had brought us so far was diminishing slowly into a soft glow. Eventually it no longer stood out from the rest of the thousand points of light. We were stuck in the middle of the desert. Worse, our messenger whom we had sent ahead, advised us that Hananias's uncle was in Alexandria and not expected to return until the spring. Balthazar suggested that we seek out King Herod and approach him about our search. If anyone should know about such a momentous event, certainly Herod should.

What a strange feeling came over us after we left Herod and his court of chief priests, scribes and hangers on. This was not the picture of someone who was excited about the prospect of a great happening about to unfold - he portrayed the image of a man with no soul, a man who would betray his brother for a harlot. We decided to be careful in any future dealings with Herod.

Bethlehem was the town of our focus now - and behold, we no sooner turned our mounts south in the direction of the town when our lost beacon of light reappeared. It moved very fast blazing across the heavens with a tail in its wake - suddenly it seemed to come to a complete stop just over the top of a hill on the outskirts of the town. We hastened to approach the spot which the heavens proclaimed as holy ground.

Many people were gathered outside a cottage next to a manger wherein we could see a donkey and a cow heavy with milk. Little lambs were scurrying in and out unmindful of their masters, the shepherds, who had pressed closer with the rest of the throng milling about to get a better look through the open shutter of the cottage. We were told that indeed a wonderful thing had happened just seven days ago - it seemed as though the sky opened up and a chorus of angels burst forth in song while a star bathed its light on the boy child born in this manger.

Shepherds from all around the hillsides came with their flocks to bear witness to this event. Soon the word spread and pilgrims and townspeople alike came to see for themselves what the angels proclaimed on high. A few days after the child was born, the family was welcomed into this cottage. Now we were told that just before we rode up on our camels, the man, Joseph, a descendant of the house of David had just returned with mother and child from the temple where according to tradition all males must undergo the rite of circumcision on the eighth day after birth. And so it was not coincidental that we three arrived on this first day of the new year to join in the celebration. The crowd made room for us to pass as we approached the cottage bearing our gifts - we stood at the doorway, just as the family following the tradition of their forefathers, raised the baby up high in the palms of their hands and announced to everyone gathered there...

"The angels of heaven have given our son his name - he shall be called Jesus."

Looking at us with tears of joy, Mary, the mother of the newborn, welcomed us as visitors from afar and beckoned us to see the baby wrapped in swaddling clothes and held close to her bosom...

The years have taught us that of all God's wonders, the miracle of birth is his greatest feat. And if this child was his chosen one which the world had been awaiting through the years, then he would be the greatest wonder of all.

With all humility, I who was born a king, went on bended knee to pay homage to the child, who came into this world as the Promised One.

"Mary, mother of Jesus," I proclaimed, "I am Melchior of Babylon. Accept this gift which I bring as a small but grateful offering from my people." I presented her with a golden chalice, forged by the best craftsman in the world, an heirloom of my family handed down for centuries as a sign of power and kingship. It was made of pure gold with emeralds fixed in a circle around the base and a large ruby placed in the center of the goblet. A gift of gold for one so noble. A gift from an earthly king to the King of Kings.

Mary bowed her head in appreciation and let me kiss the child in her arms.

Balthazar still stiff from the long camel ride hobbled in with the help of Joseph. He carried as his gift a copper urn which held white hot coals and sacred frankincense - burning away the stench of the darkness of the past to signify a fresh new beginning for mankind. A gift of fragrance for the little one. A gift from one priest to the Perfect Priest.

Gaspar took his turn with head bowed low to the ground. He moved first one knee and then the next until he was close enough to touch the hem of the blessed mother. Holding up a small hand carved wooden box in his outstretched arms, he said, "Accept this bitter-sweet gift of myrrh as a man's promise to follow the will of God yet it be sorrowful or blest with joy." A gift from just one man to the Saviour of all mankind.

Just like the chorus of angels which announced the coming of the child, each person at that special gathering sang a song of praise in his heart - a song of thanksgiving for the promise of a new beginning. This was the beauty of the child's birth. A link between our past and future to give us meaning in the present. He gave each of us a gift in return. The ability to unlock the wisdom of the heart. the power to touch someone and make him feel valued and worthwhile - be it a slave, a shepherd, soldier or king. this was a most precious gift.

With my own eyes I have seen the wonders of the world, but to witness the coming of a new world is the greatest wonder of them all.

Scott felt a calm come over him and a quiet peace. Somehow all the frustration and anxieties of career and the day to day grind faded into the background. He felt that Melchior's journal was speaking directly to him and leading him down a path which he must follow and he was not afraid.

Chapter Seventeen:

Jerusalem Revisited

everal years plus ten had gone by before we found our way back to Jerusalem again. We recalled our hurried trip to avoid Herod's troops that wondrous night, following the river Jordan north to the Sea of Galilee before turning east across the border to find the Tigris which led us back home. This time, Gaspar, Balthazar, Kunta and I were on a mission to learn more about the miracle child we witnessed years ago, and second, to assuage our guilt about never seeing the temple which Kunta built in Africa. We arrived during the annual festivities for the Passover. Hananias invited us to visit and in truth we came seeking to find out if he had made any new discoveries.

Hananias and his uncle Joram greeted us warmly. "God's blessings on you, travelers from afar," Joram said. "Welcome to our humble abode. Come in, share our meal with some friends and let us talk of many things." He introduced us to Joseph of Arimathea, Aquila from Caesarea and Pathros, a wealthy caravan merchant. We renewed old friendships that night and established new bonds.

The next day we walked to the temple to observe the celebrations. We wanted especially to listen to the famous Jewish teachers reading from the Torah even though we were not intending to participate. Upon our arrival we found a huge crowd gathered around the vestibule where the scholars convened. There standing in the middle of the throng was a young boy, poised with a confidence beyond his years, asking and answering every question put to him by a most imposing panel of judges.

We heard a bystander whisper to his companion, "Behold this young boy stands up to the oldest of the Rabbis. He chides their skepticism by quoting from the Book of Proverbs. When they complained that he asked so many questions, he answered, 'The heart of the wise seeketh instruction: and the mouth of fools feedeth on foolishness.'"

Then he boldly questioned the leader of the priests, "Why do you permit the moneychangers and merchants to take advantage of the simple folk here in the temple of the Lord?"

The priest replied, "What is it to you?" Again, he quoted from the Holy Book, "He that is greedy of gain troubleth his own house: but he that hateth bribes shall live."

Gaspar signaled us to follow him as he pushed his way through the crowd so we could get closer and hear for ourselves the lively debate which had captivated the multitude. We listened closely as he posed another question to the biblical scholars.

"Why do you choose to instill only the fear of God and not his compassion?" They did not respond. The young boy then continued, "A glad heart maketh a cheerful countenance: but by grief of mind the spirit is cast down."

One of the priests stood and shouted, "The God of our fathers is a vengeful God." Calmly, the young boy looked up to heaven and proclaimed. "Hell and destruction are before the Lord. But how much more the hearts of children of men!"

Soon one of the priests demanded to know the boy's name and where he was from. I noticed some of the King's guards coming over to see what the commotion was about so without hesitation I told Balthazar to follow my lead and advise the others to do likewise. Removing the old robes covering our Eastern garb I strode boldly into the center of the court.

"O great ones, we have traveled many miles to hear you read from the Sacred Scriptures. My friend, Balthazar, comes to ask your advice.

Balthazar caught the attention of the band of scholars and also the fancy of the crowd as they admired the brightly colored silk which HupJai had given him. Gaspar, Kunta and I surrounded the young boy and whisked him out of harm's way. He seemed unconcerned for his safety but most appreciative for our thoughtfulness.

No words needed to be said as he looked into our eyes and smiled in understanding.

"Jesus," his mother Mary called. "Jesus. We have been searching for you for three days. Joseph and I have been so worried. Why have you done this?"

We could not hear the young boy reply but we saw him hug them tightly and comfort them. Once again, we three knew that we had been in the presence of the Promised One. His time was yet to come.

The day in Jerusalem at the Synagogue was just the beginning of the ties that bound our group with the young boy whom we saw often through the years that followed. His enthusiasm for meeting the wisest men of the day from all parts of the world was contagious. We who were the teachers now became the students. And we listened with fascination as he discussed philosophy, religion, the arts, astronomy and all things great and small.

Often he would join us on caravans to attend our symposium held every year in a different location. HupJai showed him the beauty of the east sailing in a junk up the Grand Canal of China. Kunta anxiously took him to meet the elders of his homeland under warm Africa stars. Gaspar proudly guided him through the ancient seven wonders of the Mediterranean saving the pyramids for last. There in the land of the Pharaohs, his usual happy countenance seemed to grow sad as he talked of the ancient days of captivity for his people and of Moses.

Balthazar was fortunate enough to travel with him for an extended period through the Hindu mountains to the five Waters of India. They arrived back in Babylon in the fourteenth year of the reign of Tiberius Caesar. This would be the last symposium attended by the man from Nazareth who was not yet thirty in years. He announced that his time was soon at hand and he was now committed to bringing the good news to the people in his homeland. For this he was born and for this he had devoted his life.

That was the last time I saw him, the one whom the stars pointed out to us that wondrous night on a hilltop in Bethlehem.

Our friend Balthazar followed his ministry and wrote to me regarding many of the miracles performed by Jesus. I was not surprised. One letter especially touched my heart when Balthazar sent word for word his Sermon on the Mount. I read those words a hundred times over.

My old wound reopened again and not even Esther could stop the pain though she used all of her wiles and magical potions. Even as I write this, I sense that my end is near so I am rushing to finish the task I began long ago as a legacy for my descendants. Along with this journal I have entrusted my beloved wife to attach my letter of instructions and to add the lessons which I have learned throughout my life which I call the Precepts of Happiness. I am not afraid. I know that someone goes before me. I am ready to follow."

Scott had to use his magnifying glass to read the last lines inscribed in the journal. "In the eighteenth year of the reign of Tiberius Caesar, Pontius Pilate, being governor of Judea, and Herod the II being tetrach of Galilee, and Philip his brother tetrach of Iturea and Lysanias tetrach of Abilina, word came from the Magi, Gaspar of Greece, that the Nazarene had been crucified and buried that day. A second message from Gaspar came three days later with a proclamation that Jesus was risen ad asked Melchior to join him and Balthazar as quickly as possible.

A reply was sent to Gaspar and Balthazar that on the very day the first message was sent, Melchior had asked to see the sunrise for the last time. Held closely in the arms of his wife, Melchior closed his eyes in sleep as the golden rays of the sun touched the green mountains of his beloved homeland - Babylon.

Chapter Eighteen:

Melchior's last Testament

This is a collection of my manuscripts which I leave as a record of my passage through this journey we call life on earth. I leave it with all humility as an inheritance for my brethren…not to highlight any of my accomplishments but to leave the seeds of wisdom which can grow to fruition only with the passage of time…this is my wish for the generations to follow, this is my legacy…

To my beloved wife, as I entrusted you with my heart while we were together, I now bequeath to you all that I cherish…may joyful memories fill your dreams until we are reunited in the gardens of Paradise…

To my youngest child, I entrust the staff of our ancestors. On the day of my passing, you will carve your name beneath that of your father as a symbol of a new generation taking its place in the long history of our line…you will do the same for your seed when your time is ended and the circle of life is repeated…

To my eldest child, I entrust the task of keeping the family united - a heavy responsibility - and to continue the tradition of the Symposium of the Magi.

To all my children, I entrust you with the Precepts of Happiness. This is my most precious possession. It is the sum total of my life's search for meaning and my quest for the truth. All things will come and go, but with the wisdom of the Precepts you will endure. This is my gift to you. A gift more precious than gold. The Precepts of Happiness.

FOUR PRECEPTS OF HAPPINESS

1. Follow the Star
2. Climb Every Mountain
3. Hear the Voices in the Wind
4. Cherish the Tree of Life

Follow the Star

Just as we Magi followed the Star of Bethlehem which led us to the beginning of a new age, I encourage you, my sons and daughters, to use the five points of the star as a guiding light to all that you do. In order to be happy, you must take care that the core of the star burns brightly by focusing on each of the five cornerstones of life. This is the Law of nature. This is the balance that must be established.

Above all else, look to the Source of all creation. God is the eye of the universe and you must find your place in it. Every man is born into this world with a divine purpose. Seek to find that meaning. There is wisdom in the questions of the young and the old. Hear their questions. They ask the important ones. But it is not enough simply to ask the question - you must seek to know your spiritual self. This is the first cornerstone.

Once you have found a good reason to love yourself, you will be able to love others. Find your other half, then help others find theirs. Change is the signature of time. Friendships rise and fall, grow hot and cold like the seasons. Know that friends are those who weather the storms and are there waiting when the sun shines forth anew. Let kindness be the hallmark of all your relationships. Wise words my go unheeded, but a kind word is never squandered. This is the second cornerstone.

Some say you are what you do. If this be so, I encourage you to do what you like to do, everything else will fall into place. Make not your trade a hobby, but your hobby your trade. At the end of the day, you must find joy in your accomplishments. This is the third cornerstone.

Discipline your mind in the pursuit of excellence, yet train your body also in the rigors of physical strength, as it is only with a sound mind in a sound body that you will reap the benefits of your success and drink from the cup of fulfillment. This is the fourth cornerstone.

Riches give a man freedom and a responsibility to free others. Wealth in the hands of fools bears no fruit, wealth in the hands of the wise multiplies and gives rise to the freedoms every man covets. Freedom to speak his mind, freedom to worship his creed, freedom from the want of poverty and freedom from fear in all of its manifestations. This is the fifth cornerstone.

These five cornerstones are the foundations of freedom.

Climb Every Mountain

Some look up at the mountain from a distance and never accept the challenge to scale its height. Others attack the mountain straight on and stop dead in their tracks as soon as they come upon an insurmountable cliff. Some get lost in the thick underbrush and cannot find their way. Some are discouraged by the thorns and bristles which guard the rightful paths. Some are scared away by the demons they believe haunt the forests and hide in the woods.

Listen, my children, as I tell you that each mountain you come across is a blessing in disguise. Sometimes you will be able to conquer it easily. More often you will be tested and be forced to find alternate ways to the top. Sometimes you must find a mentor to guide you on the right course. Often you will have to take the lead and help your comrades find the right path. Every time you conquer one mountain there is another one waiting. But with each victory, I promise, the next hurdle is easier because you are that much stronger. Start now and the wonders of the world will be yours.

Hear the Voices in the Wind

Man in his arrogance has closed his ears to the truth. He has ignored the Laws of God and of the universe. He has forsaken the spirit of the law and mocked it's simple truth. He has debased the value of judgement and turned it into rules of court where jesters hold sway.

It need not be so. Imagine, my children, a world where no man need fear injustice of any kind. Imagine a world where man proclaims the dignity of every man and respects it. This is the code of honor which underlies the third precept.

Feel the gentle breeze as it caresses your face, listen to the night air as it hums through the trees, hear the sound of the wind blowing across the ocean. These are the voices of the wisdom of the ages. They speak to that part of the divinity which is in everyone of us. From the time we are born until the time we die, the voices comfort us in times of trouble. Listen. They will tell you the truth. There is a right way that is good, that is just, that is honorable. Hear the voices in the wind. When one comes to the crossroads, choose wisely, my children.

Cherish the Tree of Life

here are those who worship the past. There are those who live only for the future. Take care, my children, that you cultivate all the circles of life which keep the generations bound together in an inescapable chain of time. Each link is dependent on the other. Without one, the others wander aimlessly like a ship without a rudder and no destination in sight.

The roots of the tree give it stability and ground it to the past and tradition. The trunk of the tree is the mainstay and determines whether it will grow straight and true or turn into a gnarly broken limb. The fruit of the tree is the culmination of all things past and present.

My wish is that you will discover the gift which has been given to mankind above all other creatures great and small. The choice to decide one's fate at any given moment. Honor the past, yes, but let the memories of the past serve you well, learn from them. Let the excitement of your visions for the future give you the courage to face any challenge, be inspired by them. Most of all, enjoy the journey of life as I have done, and you will look back when the day is gone and be able to say I have chosen well.

Chapter Nineteen:

Epistle From Melchior

y beloved son,

I have entrusted to you my life's work in continuing the tradition of our Symposium. If you make it your mission in life, you will be rewarded tenfold:

Invite only those who are pure of heart, those who look for the good in each man, those who understand the fears which are common to all men, those who know that failure is just a stepping stone to success and those who are willing to offer hope and guidance to the best and to the worst of us.

Let not age, sex, color, occupation or creed be a barrier to your choosing. Search far and wide, from shore to shore to find those complementary personalities who will work well together. Find them, bring them together in one group and let them discover for themselves the meaning of our undertaking. Find those who dare to dream and make others dreamers too.

Let not the cynics, the nay-sayers, the pessimists and the skeptics dilute our message. Preserve our memoirs just as they are. Perpetuate the Precepts of Happiness just as they are. Let all who believe in its value, share the joy of spreading the news in their own words, in their own way. It is my hope and my prayer, that the generations that follow will bestow upon me the greatest honor of all - they will not think of me as just a man or a Babylonian King but as Melchior, the wise, he was our teacher.

Chapter Twenty:

Summation

"Scott, would you slow down, I can't understand a word you're saying," Ellen laughingly squeezed her husband's cheeks together.

"O.K. Let me start over," Scott, barely able to contain his excitement, began anew.

"We met back in the boardroom this morning as Arthur had asked and everyone greeted each other like long lost relatives who hadn't seen one another for years. Suddenly Nancy noticed that MacCary wasn't there. Believing he had chosen to leave, there was a sense of disappointment as many of us had grown fond of him even though he's a lawyer. The letdown didn't last long because MacCary came bursting into the room complaining about being stuck in the elevator and insisting that he was going to sue the Waldorf. Looking around at all our faces of disapproval, Arthur asked MacCary to stand up and give his impression of Melchior's memoirs and the lessons he had learned. Red faced, MacCary blabbered something under his breath.

Scott recounted to Ellen as best as he could remember the words that each of his colleagues spoke. MacCary may have been the first, but everyone else that followed had the same reaction.

The Precepts of Happiness struck a chord that would change their lives. Everyone felt the Precepts talked to them directly.

Arthur responded with great conviction. He shared with

us his own personal feelings about what he too had learned. He called us his "pearls of wisdom." Over the years, he said, people of many different experiences, lifestyles, educational backgrounds - all so very different, attended the Symposium - whether they were a doctor, an engineer, truck driver, or high school coach, an insurance agent, massage therapist, bellhop, salesman or beauty consultant - all had one thing in common. After reading the Precepts of Happiness they believed that they could make a difference by sharing it. One person sharing a little moment of kindness with another person. And another person. And another person. Until that kindness of spirit bursts into a wildfire which touches the hearts of so many unknown and unnamed souls. Every parent, every uncle and auntie, every brother and sister, every cousin and distant cousin teaching the values which can enhance each person's life. None of us knows when we may pass this way again.

"If there is anything good that we can do in this life," Arthur asked, "shouldn't we do it now? If you could, wouldn't you choose to make life more exciting, more beautiful, more mysterious, more wonderful, and most meaningful? The choice is yours." He closed his remarks by affirming his belief that ordinary people just like us can accomplish extraordinary things by following Melchior's "Precepts of Happiness."

One by one, each person in the group gave their commitment to Arthur to accept the challenge and continue the tradition begun two thousand years ago.

The two toned yellow and brown limousine taking the Hamiltons home to Nazareth exited the freeway and past Lehigh University. Scott continued about how Chao volunteered to host the reunion symposium in China and that she insisted that Ellen come too. He told her the Kincaids were gracious as ever and wanted him to be sure to give her their thanks for coming and wished us all the best.

Pausing briefly, Scott peered through the limousine's dividing window to make sure Hartwell wasn't paying attention. Then he whispered to Ellen.

"In all the excitement, I had forgotten to sign off when I returned my copy of the journal. Hartwell caught the omission and called me back. When I turned to the back of the book, I noticed for the first time all of the initials from previous guests at the symposium. Hartwell was standing over me so I didn't have the time to study the list but I did notice several that stood out in bold letters - fifty years apart: T.J. 1800; A.L. 1850; M.G. 1900; M.L.K. 1950."

Looking at him in disbelief, Ellen gasped, "Are you serious?" Then with a smile as bright as the snow outside, she added, "Why not? You just got to know one of the Magi."

Chapter Twenty One:

Epilogue

ne year later…

Scott had gotten an urgent message from Ellen and rushed home. He found her sitting in the family room with a fuzzy golden puppy on her lap. Giggling like a 5 year old while the puppy licked her ears, Ellen told him "Thunder" was a gift from the Kincaids.

As she handed him an envelope sealed with wax, she added, "This was also delivered by Mr. Hartwell in person for you," she said. "I knew it was important."

Sitting down before opening the envelope, Scott read…

"Dear Professor, I trust this letter finds you and your family in good spirits. You are the first person I am contacting about a new project which we are working on - an archaeological dig in Sicily. But in order to grasp the significance of this project, you must first acquaint yourself with the letters of Balthazar which are preserved in a monastery on the island of Cyprus.

Certainly, Ellen is invited to join you. Please give Hartwell your immediate reply.
Best Wishes,
Arthur"

Just as Scott finished reading, there was a knock on the door.

Finis

Reflections

Especially for your thoughts, notes, comments, questions

Reflections

Did you know the
Seven Wonders of the Ancient World?

Reflections

How many Magi were there?

Reflections

What countries were the Magi from?

Reflections

What did the gifts of the Magi symbolize?

Reflections

Was the Infant Jesus born on December 25 as we celebrate every year?

Reflections

Did Jesus have brothers and sisters?

Reflections

What countries did Jesus visit according to the
New Testament?

Reflections

What is the "green flash"?

Reflections

In the Symposium on "Love," whose story
did you like best?

Reflections

Who is your favorite Magi?

Reflections

How does Melchior find out about the Crucifixion?

Reflections

What did Jesus do from the age of 12 until he reappeared at age 30 to begin his mission?

No Greater Blessing

The journal tells the story of Balthazar, one of the Christmas Magi, who travels through distant lands to sit at the feet of the most learned men of his day so that he could absorb their teachings. The Symposia, held every three years are standing room only events as guests are eager to hear the discussion about the most important topics of the day – freedom; life and death; wealth, power

People have come to see the wise man and his colleagues from the East and most especially to catch a glimpse of the young man who accompanies them. The rumors say the young man is a king in disguise who weaves his tales in the simple language of the fable and leaves all who hear him speak in wonderment. No Greater Blessing is Balthazar's gift to the generations that follow. It talks about the ultimate freedom of choice bequeathed to everyman. It provides the light of hope that can never be extinguished. This is Baltazar's last testament. These are his words.

A Testament of Love

A 2000 year-old manuscript takes us on a historical journey that reveals the secrets of the ancients. Gaspar, continues the story of the Magi, or Wise Men, who have left a legacy for the generations to follow.

A Testament of Love is a gift of timeless devotion in a world left torn by war, chaos and fear. Gaspar leaves his manuscript to speak to all who will listen. He tells the story of all who were the closest followers of the Judean, whose mission in life was closely followed by the Magi from his birth to his crucifixion. Gaspar describes how each of his disciples sacrificed their lives for preaching the gospel: Peter, also known as Simon; Andrew, Peter's brother; James, son of Zebedee; John, James' Brother; Philip; Bartholomew; Thomas; Matthew, the tax collector; James, son of Alphaeus; Jude, also known as Thaddeus; Simon, the Zealot; Judas Iscariot*

He shares his stories from personal observation and the eyes of those who witnessed the events. This is his last testament. These are his words…